CHRISTMAS STORIES
In the Tradition of Rod Serling

The Complete Collection

ALSO BY RICHARD BARRE

The Wil Hardesty Novels

The Innocents
Bearing Secrets
The Ghosts of Morning
Blackheart Highway
Burning Moon

Other Titles

Echo Bay
Lost (coming in 2013)

CHRISTMAS STORIES
In the Tradition of Rod Serling

The Complete Collection

BY
RICHARD BARRE

Down and Out Books, LLC
3959 Van Dyke Rd, Ste. 265
Lutz, FL 33558
www.DownAndOutBooks.com

Cover design by JT Lindroos

ISBN: 193749540X

ISBN-13: 978-1-937495-40-4

CONTENTS

Foreword to
The Bargain

Michael Koryta

I vividly remember the first time I came across Richard Barre's work. It was while browsing a great independent mystery store in New York, a store now gone (a too-common qualifier when it comes to the great indie stores) and I was overwhelmed by my options. This was my favorite genre, and I was surrounded by it. Sensory overload. So I did what you could do in those days, and asked the store manager to make a recommendation. (This was a real human being, I swear, these things happened back then.)

"Who do you like?" he asked.

I began to rattle off the names, my favorite author hit list, and the clerk was nodding along, saying the names as fast I was, and guessing right along with me—Block, Lehane, Woodrell, Richard Barre...

I paused. "Not familiar with that last one."

Then came the great bookseller look, the one that sends you out the door with a full bag instead of the paperback you came in for, the one we authors depend on in a hunt for readers. I think of Jack Black in *High Fidelity* responding to browsing shoppers who hadn't heard of a particular band. That's the look, best as I can describe it.

"You haven't read Richard Barre? Well, we will fix that."

Next thing I knew, *Blackheart Highway* was in my hand. I devoured it. Barre is a master of detective fiction, of crime fiction, because he is first a master of fiction. This is a writer who cares about every sentence, not just every story. Want proof? Take a look at a quick exchange from the story you're about to read.

"You've been married long?"

"Four years. My second, her third. Daphne is her name." *Spelled M-O-N-E-Y, he decided not to add.*

There's a two-line exchange, and if it doesn't tell you what kind of writer Richard Barre is, tough and slick and funny as hell but smooth and polished, too, I can offer you another taste. Let's look at the opening, always a place where great writers knock you out and amateurs flounder:

Morning lay on Baltimore cold and dirty as three-day-old snow. Steam rose from vents and buses and whipped off the rooftops, blending with smoke and other particulates held down by the temp. Occasionally, above the horns and curses of holiday commerce, one heard the pop of icicles dislodged by a sun resembling a shriveled orange.

Wow. Can you picture the place yet? No. You can *feel* it, you can breathe it in and smell it and hear it, you're living there for as long as Barre wants to keep you there. All established in an opening paragraph. There's a part of me that hates him for it, I assure you. What I love about this is that the story is hiding there in the description—those tiny pops of icicles beneath the horns and curses of holiday commerce. The micro world of Axel, our protagonist, playing out beneath the macro world of a big city at Christmas. He's the guy, and his is the story, that nobody in that world cares about—but you will. You'll care quickly, and deeply, because in Richard Barre's hands, Axel's world will swiftly be all that matters. It's Christmas Eve, the snow masks the city, and Axel has a little money trouble and a menacing black Santa Claus with a bargain at hand. I won't tell you more than that—these are short stories, after all, and you should come at them without the jacket-copy summary. Just know that it will be a pleasure. A Richard Barre story always is. And should you find yourself in a bookstore, a knowledgeable clerk asking who you read, make sure to include his name. If you're damn lucky, you might happen across another writer like him. I know I'm still waiting.

The Bargain

Morning lay on Baltimore cold and dirty as three-day-old snow. Steam rose from vents and buses and whipped off the rooftops, blending with smoke and other particulates held down by the temperature. Occasionally, above the horns and curses of holiday commerce, one heard the pop of icicles dislodged by a sun resembling a shriveled orange.

Over by old Memorial Stadium, where Axel Maldonado had finally found a space—no way was he going to fatten the calf of the Pakistani who owned the parking garage—wind moaned through the access tunnels like the ghosts of vengeful fans conned into paying good money for some of the teams that had shown up there.

Not that anyone would be tempted to steal or even vandalize a rusting '79 Marquis, Axel thought as he humped it through the feeble lineup of tenements and struggling businesses. No, the Marquis he hung onto for the same reason he wore his old wool overcoat instead of the cashmere down here. Protective coloration. Besides, it never hurt to be reminded how far you'd come—two Caddies and a Jag his wife drove. Crying Jag, as he'd heard the shop guys deride it. Replaced in a heartbeat if his wife hadn't threatened to cut him off.

Rounding a particularly seedy block, Axel stopped for a take-out coffee at the Puerto Rican spot he favored not because of their shared nationality, but because it was half a block down from his destination. His first apartment building, the cornice thing reading "1898" when you could make it out through the grime. Hard for Axel not to get a bit sentimental.

After all, it was his first slated for demolition.

But that wasn't until January something, December fourteenth now. Meantime, the city was still in the process of relocating his tenants with the same speed it put up Christmas decorations down here. After six months, only a few remained—last dogs in the pound. Made him want to grind his teeth, the whole process. First the preservationists, then the do-gooders and activist groups howling about tenant rights. As if those barely able to get out of bed on a good day had some right to what he'd worked his butt off for. Then the city, of course, dissing him about how anybody could actually *live* in it, their attorneys trying to keep the price down. Big show of concern that for a hundred years had basically amounted to sucking up the property taxes.

Politics, he thought as he stopped walking to look up at it.

Like most buildings on the block, his had the usual posse of first-and second-floor businesses: video arcade, welfare dentist, passport photo establishment, a place that carved lamb off a spit. And on five, *his* office, converted from the niche that had been a supply closet down from where his manager had lived.

Axel's eyes took in brick exterior, iron ladders and landings clinging to it, grillwork dripping rust-tinged ice. And in the windows rising to the ninth floor: sun-faded sheets, taped-up newspapers, psychedelic wrapping paper, old rock posters.

Humanity, he breathed, stepping back for a better angle on a spray-canned bit of graffiti that wasn't there last week. *Fuck This Shit* in wild scrawl.

Same to you mother—

"Hey, who you backin' into?"

Axel turned at the bump, saw one of the Santas they had all over the place: tin pot swinging from a collapsible tripod, little bell in his big hand. Axel in his concentration not having heard the thing.

"Who are you?" he asked.

"Who you see—Perry Como?" Big black dude poured into his red-and-white costume, dangly hat with its cotton snowball on the end. Phony-looking long white beard stuck to his chin.

"No," Axel said. "I mean where's the regular guy? Arnie."

"Ernie. Man got himself the wrong side of some Chateau Lafite or something. I'm filling in."

Right about that, Axel thought—Ernie, this tall skinny guy looked like the wind could blow clear to D.C. Three sheets to it most of the time.

But at least he more or less fit the profile.

"Nice neighborhood," Santa said, glancing upward. "Livin' large."

"What's that supposed to mean?"

"Three guesses. And don't think I don't recognize you, either. You the guy owns this dump."

"What did you say?"

"You heard me. Ernie described you, right down to the overcoat. Middle-aged, balding Puerto Rican trying to dress down, blend in. Said you was usually good for a donation, though."

"Ernie said that—like I'm supposed to cough up every time I see one of you people?"

"Hey, now. Don't hear me callin' *you* names."

"I meant the costume and beard," Axel said, not wanting trouble. One call and the place is crawling with sign wavers, all of them calling a man's pedigree into question if not his motives. Welcome to the loony bin.

"Speaking of which," *Santa Negro* was saying. "Seems like you nearly crash into a guy, you'd want to make amends. Specially if Santa's the crashee."

Madre de Dios. Axel checked his watch: places to go and already coming up on ten o'clock. He reached into his overcoat, through it and into his pants pocket. Palming some change, he held it over the slot and released, the coins clinking off the pot's bottom.

"Fifty lousy cents?"

Axel, on his way to the doorway that led to the stairwell, turned. "Now what?"

"*Clink-clink?* You think Santy don't know you been naughty or nice?"

"I don't believe this."

"You don't believe it? Got people livin' in your building treat this thing with more respect."

Axel reached in again, hoping the bill he was feeling around for was the dollar he remembered from dressing, when Santa said, "No way. How many chances you think you get in life?"

That stopped him. "Time out. You're saying now you don't want a donation?"

"That's what I'm saying. Just don't blame me when the roll is called up yonder. Eye of the needle, remember?"

Axel was shaking his head and muttering under his breath about the people they let out to work this job, half tempted to make his own call about this nut—even scarecrow Ernie looking good about now—when Santa said, "Got an idea, Mr. Landlord." Nodding now. "Second chance, as it were."

A bargain, Axel thought as he settled into his cubbyhole office—desk he had his feet up on, phone he could disconnect and store in the lockable filing cabinet, big deadbolt on the heavy windowless door he had propped open. The whole fifth floor feeling weird from nobody being on it, smelling now like any combination of things, piss and cabbage right up there. Standard interior decor with these people.

But a bargain offered by a six-two, three-hundred-pound black Santa had it all beat.

"This the way it works," he'd said. "Seeing as you so poor and all, you get to keep half."

"Half. Of what?"

"Of whatever falls in your pocket today. That's my part of the bargain. Your part is to share half."

Axel dodged street splash. "Share...with you?"

"With the pot. Chance to redeem yourself with old Santy."

"And I keep the other half."

"You hard of hearing?"

"Try this," Axel said. "Just in case something *remotely* like that happens, what's to prevent me from keeping the whole thing?"

"Nothin'."

"Some bargain."

Santa just smiled. "What's to lose?"

"Deals in place or tax refunds, forget it," Axel said hastily to cover that loophole. Nothing personal, just business. Still, he felt sheepish about the fifty cents. Less for having given it than for getting called on it by this weirdo.

"Done." Santa said.

As they shook on it, Axel fought the feeling that his remaining tenants might be watching, getting the wrong idea about him. Even worse, the business owners, last to leave under the agreement. Like he'd gone soft—become some pushover they could dick around.

Safely inside now, he leaned back in the swivel chair there when he'd bought the place. Three other locations collecting rent and the settlement on this one decent enough to buy him an office building he had his eye on.

Bargain with Santa, my ass, he thought, planting his feet on the floor. Luckily, there was a back entrance.

For the next two hours, Axel caught up on the reams of paperwork every government agency from city to federal required. He was finishing his coffee, long cold by now, when the phone rang.

"Mr. Maldonado?" A mature female voice. Pleasant enough, but you couldn't be too careful.

"Who's this?"

"Hazel Lokesh, Housing & Redevelopment. Calling to wish you happy holidays on behalf of the city."

Here we go. "I'm sorry, Ms. Lokesh, but—"

"Mrs. Lokesh."

"Who can keep track anymore? And yes, you've caught me at a bad time."

"Before you hang up, Mr. Maldonado, please hear me out."

"If it's about the agreement, I'd advise you to contact my lawyer. His name is—"

"I'm quite familiar with Mr. D'Avila, thank you. This needn't involve him. It's about an offer we're prepared to make."

"You condemn my building and now you want to make me an offer."

Instead of rising to it, she replied, "We both know you received fair value, Mr. Maldonado. And the offer comes through me from another agency."

Just in case the evil slumlord needs some muscling, Axel thought. Still, she was right about the settlement. They both knew that. "You have five minutes before I have to be somewhere."

"They're prepared to pay for the furnished shelter of one Mary León, age eighty-four. Not beyond the first of the year."

Axel drew a breath, regarded the paperwork spread out on his desk. "Tell me," he said. "What kind of a name is León?"

There was a pause. "Puerto Rican. I would have thought—"

"Just wanted to hear you say it, Mrs. Lokesh. Spics to the spics, right?"

"I won't dignify that."

For a moment neither spoke.

"What kind of money we talking?"

"One thousand dollars."

About twice his monthly rental rate for a one-bath studio—under ordinary circumstances. He tapped his pencil. "I don't think so, but thanks."

"Mr. Maldonado, we happen to know you have the better part of a building available when nothing else is right now."

"Interesting you'd say that. Aren't you the people who tear these places down to prove you hate people like me?"

"One relationless, indigent woman. Every approved option either at maximum or unavailable until the first."

"In the whole city..."

"Unusually high demand, Mr. Maldonado, brought on by a combination of factors, this weather among them. What possible harm..."

"Keep open an empty health hazard, as your lawyers put it, for next to nothing? If that's all, Mrs. Lokesh, good-bye."

Axel hung up. Ten minutes later, as he was preparing to go out—via the rear—the phone rang.

"Two thousand," she said without preamble. "Heat included."

"Twenty-five hundred."

There was a long sigh. "You know, I'm looking over our agreement with you, and I—"

"But you won't," he said. "Not for a mere twenty-five hundred. In advance."

Another pause. "And a rollaway bed for her attendant—to ensure your noninvolvement, of course."

Axel gave it a few seconds to let her know who she was dealing with. "For that amount, I suppose. Long as it's one room."

"Very well. We'll be moving Mrs. León in tomorrow if there'll be someone there. Would that be you, Mr. Maldonado?"

"It would, Mrs. Lokesh. Nine sharp. No tricks, though: for sure somebody takes her after the first?"

"That is correct."

"Comfort me on that. Who takes her?"

"A bed is coming open at one of the convalescent hospitals."

"What—she's sick?"

"Nothing contagious, Mr. Maldonado. And now, I bid you good day."

"Trying to lay some guilt trip on you, that's all," Daphne said.

He was home now, already having called his attorney, Phil D'Avila, Phil agreeing he could go at it head-on if he chose, but calling it lose-lose if the press got wind, which could easily be this do-gooder's ace in the hole. After all there *was* the issue of the season: SLUMLORD TURNS MARY AWAY— AGAIN. Agenda-driven garbage like that.

"Like they say, just say no," Daphne said for about the tenth time, trying to cheer him up. Axel nursing a drink and watching Daphne model the stuff she'd bought downtown while he was getting it handed to him by the Lokesh woman.

"It's not like these people got any respect for you as a person," Daphne slipping on a little something looked as if it ought to cost about $8.95 but was probably fifty times that. "You know I'm right, baby. I mean, aren't they supposed to give two weeks' notice or something?"

Axel rose from the chaise and poured himself another Scotch—a double this time.

At nine the next morning, sky looking as if it hadn't bothered to get up—let alone that Santa, who thankfully was nowhere in sight—a van pulled to the curb in front of Axel's building. One of those ramp-adapted things that let wheelchairs out to get in everybody's way.

Axel left the shelter of the doorway and went to meet the person getting out the passenger's side. Through the side windows, he could see white hair and a young woman beginning to gather up some things.

"Mr. Maldonado? Hazel Lokesh."

Large dark eyes, *café con leche* skin, cropped black hair with threads of gray: not bad looking overall. "You bring payment with you?" he asked.

She handed him a check-window envelope that he pocketed as they stood watching the lift deposit the chair woman and her attendant on the sidewalk. The attendant's eyes already flashing on the video arcade sign.

Axel concentrated on Mary León. She looked okay, he thought—at least upright in her chair. But then he saw her eyes...as if they were looking inside instead of out as they brought her to the elevator and up to the studio he'd set in order. Floor five, where his office was. Minimize the heat and electricity that way.

As the driver wheeled her in, everybody but Axel looking around at dingy kitchenette, worn sofa set with chipped ceramic lamp where the pieces L'd, coffee table with duct tape holding the laminate together, pull-down and roll-away bed crowding the layout, Axel was regarding the younger woman. The one introduced as Mary León's personal attendant. Chandra—popping gum and peering out the window.

Wondering about her.

Mrs. Lokesh knelt down beside the wheelchair and removed the blanket from Mary León's blue bathrobe. Patting her hand, she said, "Isn't this pleasant?"

Axel had never heard any of his units referred to that way, but he wasn't about to argue.

"Oh, yes," Mary said. "Very nice." Surprising Axel—not exactly knowing what to expect from someone in that state. Nothing like Daphne's mother. Lord, *that* whole thing...

Mrs. Lokesh was waving him over. "This is Mr. Maldonado," she said. "He owns the building."

Mary extended a frail hand that showed surprising grip. But something wasn't right—the eyes again. Like there was a physical problem with them.

"Thank you for having me on such short notice, Mr. Maldonado. It's good of you to take an old person in."

"My pleasure, ma'am," Axel said, feeling the check crinkle in his pocket as he leaned back. Involuntarily placing a hand over it at the glance from Mrs. Lokesh.

Out in the hall, Chandra stowing Mary's few things and the driver back downstairs, Mrs. Lokesh said, "As I'm sure you can tell, she eats very little—canned nutrient, mostly. You saw the cans?"

Axel nodded.

"Another thing: Her vision is on and off, mostly off."

"Just what's wrong with her?"

"A form of brain cancer. Rare and inoperable."

Great. "Anything else?"

"She has a tendency to confuse people with a son she's never given up hope over. Rudy. Don't take it personally."

"I won't."

"We tried locating him, without success. She has pictures of him as a child, but they're of no help now."

"She's dying, isn't she?"

"We're all dying, Mr. Maldonado."

"Don't give me that. She even going to make it till the first?"

"I don't know."

"Truth or the deal's off."

"You'd throw her out in the street?"

"I don't have problems enough, Mrs. Lokesh? You tricked me."

"How? She could go tomorrow or a month from now. Either way, you win." Looking at the peeling wallpaper and burned-out hall lights, the threadbare runner and soiled wood, she added, "We do what we can, Mr. Maldonado."

Axel took a breath. "What about if she—"

"Dies? Her doctor says it should be quite minimal. She'll just...go. His name is Doctor Singh, by the way. You'll see him if you're around."

Axel made note of it, also taking down phone numbers, one where Singh could be reached after hours.

"Do as I do," Mrs. Lokesh added. "Think of her as nearly out. I find it helps a great deal in my line of work."

Next morning, after depositing the check, Axel was in his office when Dr. Singh stopped by, Axel finding him a pleasant enough sort.

"Not great," Singh replied when Axel inquired, the man clearly waiting for him to ask. "She's a tough old bird, even though it's wearing her down."

"So far, so good, in other words."

"Stop in and see her if you like. She still responds to visitors."

Right, he thought. *Put it on the schedule.*

An hour and a half after Singh left, Chandra having followed him down in the elevator, Axel played a hunch, took the stairs to the video arcade. And there she was: hard at one of the games, stack of quarters beside her, and three young men her age egging her on. Lost in it.

So what, Axel thought—*somebody else's problem.* He was about to dip out, get a sandwich or something he could eat at his desk, when he paused, let himself be drawn back upstairs.

Chandra had left the door open, and Mary was in her wheelchair at the window, where part of the newspaper had been torn away to reveal begrimed glass and brick. Begrimed city. She was so still, Axel was afraid he'd jolt her by speaking.

He was easing the door shut, not wanting her to start roaming the halls, when she said, "Rudy? Is that you?"

Don't say you weren't warned. "No, ma'am. Axel Maldonado. Sorry to bother you."

Without moving her head, she raised a hand toward him.

"Come sit by me," she said.

"I really can't, I was on my way to—"

"Please..."

Axel pulled over the one chair that looked as if it might support him.

"The view is lovely, don't you think, Mr. Maldonado?"

"Well, it..."

"I love the spring so much. All the flowers blooming."

That did it. He was about to beg off, when she said, "Of course I know it's winter, I just pretend it isn't. Sometimes that's all one can do."

Axel settled onto a split in the vinyl.

"You have children?"

"Never had the time. Besides, my wife—" *Jeez—where was this coming from?*

"What about her?"

"Put it this way—she has her interests."

"You've been married long?"

"Four years. My second, her third. Daphne is her name." *Spelled M-O-N-E-Y,* he decided not to add.

"Such a pretty name. She must be very proud you own such a fine building."

Axel said nothing.

"You know, I don't know whether they told you, but my son Rudy will be coming. That's who I thought you were at first, though I can see now that you don't look anything like him."

Don't do this, he thought. Then: *What the hell, who had to know?* "What was he like, your son?"

She defocused before his eyes. With a smile, she said, "Strong and handsome. Dark hair like his father, who fought against Franco. Are you old enough to remember that time at all?"

"I remember my uncle saying things about the Spanish Civil War. Relatives he had in it or something."

Her face went back to the window. "Rudy went away like that, but he'll be back by Christmas. You'll see him."

For a while, they sat in silence, Axel still wondering what the hell he was doing there in nutsville: empty floor in a near-empty flophouse with this near-empty old woman.

"Such a nice view from here," Mary León said at length.

"If you say so," Axel found himself mumbling.

Late afternoon, Chandra still not back, Axel checked in again and found Mary León slumped over in her chair. He was feeling for pulse, his own heart racing, thoughts going every which way, when she mumbled, "So hard to sleep sitting up. Could you please put me in bed?"

After a moment's fumbling, he had the leverage and lifted her over, light even in her heavy robe. "Thank you, Mr. Maldonado," she said, Axel not even aware she'd opened her eyes.

In what seemed like seconds, she was asleep.

Axel retrieved the push-out blade he'd brought and quietly removed the remaining newspaper from the window, then used the spray cleaner and a roll of paper towels he'd left at the door. Half an hour of straining and maneuvering, silent cursing and balancing, the window was clean.

Glad nobody had seen it and relatively pleased at the results, he turned to find Chandra staring at him. Walkman strapped to her waist, its headphones hanging off her neck and down her back. Thumpy rock 'n' roll coming through all the way from there.

With a smirk, she said, "Do that for all your tenants?"

Axel grabbed her elbow and spun her into the hall. "Deal," he said, with heat. "You shut up about this, I don't report you for negligence."

"Go ahead," she said shrugging. "See if I care. You think I like doin' this—crazy old dyin' woman in *this* hole? Gotta be crazy yourself just to be around her." She jerked free, went inside, came out with an open can of Mary León's nutrient she held under his nose. "Try smellin' that all day, you wonder why I go downstairs. Enough to make you gag."

At home that night—Daphne with friends, according to her note—Axel rummaged and found a still-boxed radio she'd purchased six of on a whim. Her lucky number or something. Thinking this far and no further, he put the box in the Marquis with the fruit he'd picked up—tangerines from South Africa and priced accordingly. Just so he could say he'd done something for his money in case it came up. Which it always could.

At ten he turned in, watched the news for as long as he could stand, then snapped off the light. And when Daphne rolled in at half-past midnight, thunking her shoes into the closet, humming and swilling mouthwash in the bathroom, Axel was still staring up at the darkness.

On the morning of the twenty-first, a week after the Santa incident Axel had done his best to forget, the last of the tenants moved out per schedule. Finally killing power and heat to those floors, Axel found himself thinking more and more about the bargain with Old Weirdo. Particularly about splitting his hard-earned cash—especially under circumstances that were requiring more of his time by far than he'd built in. If this even *qualified.*

There was only one thing to do, and that was tell Mary León his visits of the last few days were over. *Finito.* Way too busy to sit peeling tangerines and explaining what was outside the window, listening to her stories about Puerto Rico. Something they at least had in common. But busy was the truth, all his other managers pestering him to come around and solve their problems.

Only his life.

Mary was at her daily post by the window when he stepped in at her response to his knock. Chandra, naturally, had stepped out.

"It's a fine morning, Mr. Maldonado," Mary said, her eyes not quite finding him where he stood. Never mind the fact that it had started snowing, everything beyond the glass vague at best. "And I can't tell you what a difference the radio has made."

Just your basic $350 Bose Wave in the background. "You eat this morning, ma'am?"

"Please call me Mary."

Answer enough, Axel thought, the smell Chandra had familiarized him with like a silent scream. Empty cans in the trash adding to it.

Axel sealed the plastic liner and set it out in the hall—which gave him a chance to take the cellophane off the box he'd brought.

"Thought you might like these," he said, sitting and handing her one.

She grasped it, smelled, tasted.

"Chocolate," she said. "Real *chocolate.*"

"Didn't want it to go to waste."

She savored it. "You know, I was wrong, Mr. Maldonado. You do remind me of him—of Rudy I mean. See, I have to remember that he was no more than a boy when he went away."

Axel said nothing, curiously rooted to the cushion he'd found at a Salvadoran *tienda.* Little brighter than he went for, but priced right.

"Tell me about your family," she said.

"Not much to tell. No father. Mother gave me up to a sister who disowned me later to marry some guy who had other plans. Joined the navy, served two terms, wound up here."

A smile dawned. "And look how well you've done. A nice place like this—"

"Ma'am—Mary." About up to here with all of it, himself included. "It's time you knew. This place isn't nice at all, it's a trash heap. Even Santa Claus said so. Coupla weeks they're going to knock it down and haul it off."

Mary León sat very still. "After I'm gone, I hope."

Shit. Shit, shit, shit. It was this damned snow on top of everything else. This whole situation. "I'm sorry. I didn't mean—"

"It's all right. Going blind heightens the other senses, or so they say. They...I wonder who *they* are. Have you ever wondered that—they who tell us these things?"

"I should go," he said. "Not add to your problems."

"What problems, Mr. Maldonado? Haven't you been listening? My son is coming—Christmas eve—I know it now. A mother knows when her son is close." Smiling directly at him, this time as if she *could* see inside.

Dr. Singh dropped by at eleven the next morning. "Just so you know, she's failing. She'll be lucky to make Christmas."

Axel had noticed the cans of nutrient were full when he'd gone to check on her, still sleeping. Which verified what Chandra had said about her not eating before the girl had gone home with cramps or something. Back when she felt like it, Axel supposed.

"So what do I do?" he said in a voice that didn't sound like his.

"Nothing you can do, Mr. Maldonado. You have my number?"

Axel nodded, *Nothing you can do* still echoing.

For a while he just sat there, putting a wall around it. Then he got up and slowly walked through the motes of dust spinning in the glare from the far window, to her room.

Mary was still asleep. Watching the covers rise and fall, Axel spotted a wood box beside her hand, gently lifted it away.

Inside were black-and-white photographs turning brown...roughly two dozen of them, some showing the inside of a house, others the outside...a beautiful young woman who had to be Mary...Mary with another young man and woman—sister and brother from the resemblance and way their arms rested easily on one another. But most were of Mary with a baby who grew in subsequent shots into a handsome dark-haired youth of four or five.

For whatever reason, there the shots ended.

They were so familiar looking...as if he were looking into his own past. But that was ridiculous, the product of the tropical-looking foliage that framed them. Still, they set up a resonance in him he thought Mary must surely hear before he put back the box, reached the safety of his office, and shut the door.

It was three o'clock before he even looked at his watch.

Five before he was off the phone.

They came the next day, the twenty-third—directed by Axel to the larger unit next door—the one he'd opened the radiators in early that morning after having slept in the rollaway. Hoping now that as he lifted Mary out of bed and sat with her at the window, she wouldn't be aware of the noise.

She didn't seem to be, a smile lingering on her face at just about every opportunity except when he offered her the nutrient. Taking a little of the chicken soup he'd thought to bring up from the Greek place, but only a little.

And they talked between her naps, Axel aware about midday that they'd lapsed into Spanish. About Rudy almost exclusively now: what she thought he'd look like, if he'd recognize her, not wanting to be in the bathrobe when he came, her few items of clothing stuffed into the travel bag Chandra had crammed into the closet.

She'd drifted again into sleep when the last of the workmen finished up at one A.M., Axel cutting him a check on the spot. Like the others, holiday rate, double overtime. Heart Attack Hotel at some other time.

Axel went back and fell asleep watching the snow mask Baltimore.

He awoke at five-thirty with a stiff neck, checked to see she'd made it through the night, then sorted out the rest of the day over instant Folger's reconstituted on his office hot plate.

Christmas Eve—the most bizarre of his life. Nothing else even close.

At least the room was ready. Except for the thing he'd been too tired to accomplish the night before.

Taking the rolled posters, he slipped into the next-door apartment and taped them carefully to the window, then stood back to survey the effect, "Silver Bells" playing softly on the Bose. The team had done its best to match the old-fashioned furniture in the photograph and had come pretty close, Axel thought, comparing it to the shot from the box they'd used. Of course the new wallpaper wasn't quite right, and the holly and the candles, the swoops of paper chains, the Christmas tree with its icicles and angels and twinkling lights didn't exactly mesh thematically with the tulips and daffodils now in the window, but hey—how real was it in the streets? How real was any of it?

Him? Here? Now? Like this?

Daphne'd have him committed.

Ten days ago, *he'd* have had him committed.

Mary was sitting up in bed when he came back. He helped her put on what she wanted over her thin nightgown: a floral-patterned housedress and fringed shawl Axel recognized from one of her pictures. She even took in more of the chicken soup he warmed as they reminisced about Puerto Rico.

At noon he told her he had a surprise and wheeled her next door.

By three o'clock, Mary's eyes had become nearly useless from all they'd seen and joyously commented on, finally closing "to save my strength," as she put it. "Besides, what more *can* I see after Christmas in spring in my own home?" Axel feeling something he'd never felt as he lifted her into the new bed with the down comforter. Not recognizing what it was; not even making the attempt.

He was looking around the room as she napped, five-fifteen and almost dark, wondering what the rest of the building would have been like this way—really nice—when she reached out to him.

Her hand was ice cold.

As he leaned over to warm it in both of his, to say it was all right—that everything would be all right, and of course it was Rudy, Rudy was there, *Merry Christmas, Madre*—she said, "I knew it was you the whole time, *corazón*." Opening her eyes and finding him. "Didn't you?"

Then she was gone. Just as Dr. Singh had predicted. He'd been wrong about one thing, however, Axel thought with hot tears and hotter pride. Mary León's death had not been minimal, was not minimal.

Her smile told him that much.

He'd been staring at it for however long, marveling at how much younger her face looked in death, when there was a knock and Mrs. Lokesh entered. She was about to add something to "I've been calling all *day*," when she fell silent, open-mouthed at the room. She was still gaping as Axel raised himself off Mary León's bed and walked back to his office.

Stars were out when Axel finally emerged on the sidewalk, and the breeze was fresh from the north, a good sign for tomorrow. Down the block a few lights were up, mainly in the storefronts. Not many people were out Christmas Eve.

But some were.

"Saw you from the window," Axel said, his breath pluming. "Thought you'd packed it in."

"I look the type?"

"Kind of late in the game."

Santa Negro lowered his bell. "Still a few hours left. You never can tell."

"Who are you?"

"You ain't got eyes?"

"I mean really."

"Long story. Does it matter?"

Axel stared at him a few seconds, then shrugged. "No, I suppose not." Turning up his collar against the cold.

"Been waiting to see if you're gonna honor your part of the bargain. Half to the pot—remember?"

"What makes you think I'd give half even there was half?"

The man smiled. "First to admit, I got my doubts."

Axel felt in his pants pocket, found the check he'd written—$2500 made out to Cash. "Don't feel bad," he said, crunching across to the pot. Slipping the check into it. "Some people just are who they are."

Foreword to
The Star

Michael Connelly

I used to be against them. I used to have a chip on my shoulder. I was biased. I was even prejudiced. I'm talking about the short story. I didn't write them, I didn't read them. At least since I'd become a so-called professional. My thinking was that if an idea or a character or even both weren't worth a good 300 pages of exploration then they just weren't worth my time. Plain and simple, but that's the way it was.

That was then and this is now. I am reformed now. I'm in the church. A few years ago my so-called professional responsibilities brought me to the collected works of Edgar Allan Poe. The big man himself. The master. And of course, his work is shot through with the short form. I had read these stories before. Many of them. In my early years—before I took on the mantle of the professional writer. I thought reading them again would be a chore. But I was very wrong. Reading them again was like coming home to the things that made me want to become a professional. It was like being baptized in sacred waters. I saw the light.

Or rather, I saw the power. I understood again the secret of how less could be more. How in economy there is craft and no brevity of important and moving ideas. I knew that the short story had the power of all the emotions. The power to pierce, to tug, to scare. To make one think and feel something new.

Like all biases, mine was stupid and born of ignorance. I am over that now. I now try my hand in the same fields plowed so nobly by people like Poe. I am far behind but not deterred.

Richard Barre is not far behind. He has known the secret for a long time. He's plowed this field before and his rows are nice and straight. This story reminds me of Poe in many ways. A house with an aura, a cloak of the seemingly sinister underworld. A man of intrigue and mystery. A young person full of curiosity and hope. There is a spooky polish rubbed over all of this, onto every surface until it shines. Barre knows what he is doing and this story shows it. Edgar would be proud because it ripples with the muscle of less being more.

The Star

I went back the other day.

No reason, really, other than it had been a while. Maybe it was the weather, one of those hazy days after Thanksgiving that make L.A. seem as if it's still smoldering from the fire season...like a pile of leaves being consumed without flames, the smoke rising up around the streetlights and making your eyes water.

The way it used to be when Marshalk lived in the house.

I sat looking at it in the twilight. It was always sort of a mongrel—Southwest plaster and tile slapped onto a late-teens California bungalow, the kind with the open-book roof jutting out to create a porch where occupants might watch the neighbors and relish an evening breeze, such as there was. But somewhere in the thirties this one had caught Santa Fe fever and the result was, well, unusual—the best or worst of both styles, I couldn't tell which. At any rate, with its double-lot width and protruding front window, it stood out among the singles and twenties-vintage clapboards around it.

Especially in 1953. When I was twelve and we lived next door.

Me, Naomi, and Mama.

I lit a cigarette with the car lighter and squinted out through the smoke. What used to be ours was gone now, knocked down and rebuilt to look like something that might house a large pair of shoes. But that wasn't why I was there...

My eyes went back to the Marshalk place.

I was glad I hadn't come during the day; with no lights on, the house's age receded as though mercifully veiled. Gaps showed in the curving tile roof. A realtor's sign stuck up near the front window, barred now, reflecting the times. Cracks laced the stucco facade, and on one wall some lunkhead had sprayed a homeboy slogan. Beside the drive, the giant deodar, once so full and droopy, looked stark against the twilight sky.

Which reminded me.

I looked up, searching for the star, but it wasn't dark enough to see yet. That was okay, I could wait. And remember.

"Byron Whitaker, you get in this house right now."

"Maa—it's still light." Mothers. I tried again: "Lukie and Clifford's mom lets them—"

"You want me to tan your hide in fronta the neighbors?" The ultimate threat, even though I could outrun her. Still, I had to eat sometime, and she knew it. Speed didn't count for beans then.

"Lydell and Chondra invited me to come watch TV," I said, knowing I was done but hoping for deliverance. Everybody I knew had a TV, surely everyone in Leimert Park.

Everyone but us.

"There's gonna be a Christmas special on—"

"Gonna be one sorry boy on this block in about one minute."

"Coming," I said in my most devastated voice.

"Nighty night, Byron," the gaggle of kids intoned to my back. "By—ron."

I trudged up the stairs, banged the screen and slumped into a kitchen chair. Mama was feeding Naomi something from a jar that made her mouth orange. The baby's big dark eyes regarded me for a second then looked to the spoon for more. Her stumpy pigtails were tied off with little ribbons, making her face appear round. I sniffed, scanned the stove: tomato soup and cheese sandwiches again.

"Damn, Mama, see what you done now. Kids think I'm a baby."

"Who you hanging out with, talkin' like that?" she said without taking her eyes off Naomi. "And don't gimme that look, neither. We don't cuss in this house."

I wiped my face on my T-shirt sleeve, kickball sweat smudging dirt already there. Clearly there was no reasoning with this woman, not since Daddy left. For all I knew, I'd been switched at birth—I mean look at how much lighter my skin was than hers, the way she hounded me constantly. Made sense when you thought about it.

"I see you playing in the Marshalk yard?"

"No, Mama. Just looking for the ball." I'd hoped it wasn't that obvious, what I was up to, but there it was. A little flutter ran through me.

"Don't lie. One more time and your Daddy's gonna hear about it. You'll really get it then."

"Oh, Mama, Daddy's gone for good and you know it. Why else you workin' down at Johnson's?"

Johnson's Market needed black checkers to make the neighborhood's increasing number of Negro customers feel comfortable, and Mama applied and was hired. Week nights, she pulled evening shifts after cafeteria work at Audubon School. Which I swear was her way of keeping me in her gunsights, seeing who I was eating with, if I'd finished my lunch, stuff like that. The eyes of a hawk, that woman. Disposition too, lately.

"Why? So you can eat good and still be ungrateful." She ladled the soup into a bowl, handed it to me on a plate with my cheese sandwich cut into quarters.

I blew on the soup, spooned it around.

"You keep away from Marshalk's, the man ain't well. Mr. Titus said so. Are you listening, Byron? I'm serious."

"Yes, ma'am."

As she talked, she kept one eye on Naomi, who was fussing and grabbing for a bite of sandwich. At fifteen months, Naomi was my personal cross—my responsibility to pick up from the Cooley's where she spent the day, then take care of until Mama got home at eleven on weeknights.

"Mind your sister good tomorrow, I think she's coming down with something. You done your homework yet?"

"No, ma'am. Left it for tonight so it'll be fresh in my mind Monday. Good thinking, huh?"

She shook her head slowly. "Think about this, little man. Dishes, homework, bath, bed—in that order. Are we clear on that?"

I nodded, wondering how hard it would be to find my dad once I set out to, once I got the money. No worse than living here, that was certain. Feeling like I couldn't breathe.

Not long now, I told myself. Later on, lying under the covers, my eyes open in the dark and hearing Mama's snores, I thought about how it was going to play out with Marvin Hall, Artie Bingham, and Raymo Combes. My co-conspirators.

The plan was to go over the back wall at ten. That way Naomi'd be asleep and I'd be out with the money before Mama got home. We all knew it was in there somewhere. Had to be, a house that big, Marvin said. Gold too, likely. Whole bags of it.

Setting out for school, I eyed the Marshalk place, no way of seeing in because the drapes were pulled, like always. The outside was white and unlived-in looking, with none of the Christmas decorations other houses had. Titus's car wasn't there yet, but it would be—Mondays he did light housekeeping and cooked. Mama knew this because she sold Titus his groceries, him smiling at her while she rang up the prices and put 'em in bags, her smiling back at him.

Made me want to throw up when I saw it.

Nobody ever saw Mr. Ludwig Marshalk, though. Artie thought he was dead or that Titus had him locked up in there to get his money. But Titus wasn't there at night when the house was dark. That's all we had to know.

Raymo kept saying I'd be scared. But who'd be scared of somebody named Ludwig. Somebody I'd never even seen.

"Hey, punk." Marvin surprised me as I passed an alleyway near the school. He was tall, three years older than me, and long out of Audubon. Supposed to be going to Crenshaw High—when he felt like it, I guess. Didn't have a father either, something I could appreciate even though Marvin was kind of a bully and got in fights. But who better to have on your side?

Anyway, Marvin spent most of his time smoking the cigs he kept in his rolled-up sleeves, taking money off the younger kids, and hanging out with Artie and Raymo. Who emerged behind him.

"Look who's here," Artie said. "Lord By-ron." Artie was a year behind Marvin at Crenshaw and Raymo was a grade ahead of me at Audubon, which was my connection. Lord Byron was a white wrestler who wore tights and stuff in the ring.

Artie nailed me one on the shoulder, but I didn't rub. I mean that was Artie, strong as a bear and built like one. Raymo was more my size, slight, with eyes that kept going back and forth between Marvin and Artie.

"Lord By-ron," he echoed. He giggled, amused with himself—like a girl, I thought, but didn't say anything. See, Raymo had a switchblade.

"Shut up, Ray." Marvin glowered at me. "You tell anybody about tonight, punk?"

"Hey, I ain't no snitch."

"You scared, By-ron?" Artie said.

"Take more than that."

Marvin waved Artie off. "You straight on this, Byron? You're inside the basement window, you unlock the back door, we take it from there. You got that?" Marvin pinched my shoulder muscle where it met my neck.

"Yes," I let out.

"Like takin' candy from a sleeping baby," he said, letting me go.

"What you gonna do with your share, By-ron?"

Before I could answer Raymo, Marvin said, "Gonna find his old man, aren't you Byron?" A strange light came into his eyes. "You guys believe that? What a waste. Tell him about your old man, moron. About him and your sister."

"Come on, Marvin," Raymo whined. "And don't call me moron, okay? I don't like it."

Marvin's punch was so quick I didn't even see it. But there was Raymo, doubled up on the ground and gasping.

"Sure, fool," Marvin said, winking at us. "Anything you say."

Artie laughed like crazy, but I noticed he stayed out of range.

***

So they might not have been pals exactly. But a man had to put aside childish things if he was ever going to grow up, right? If I was ever going to find Daddy and live with him, I needed the cash to do it. As Artie said once, money talks and bullshit walks. Everything would fall into place once I got the means.

School dragged by. At recess, I saw Raymo over by the fence, but I kept my distance and so did he. Afterward, I took the long way home so's not to get distracted by the other kids, then I was picking up Naomi at the Cooley's.

"She's fussy today. Got a drippy nose, too," Mrs. Cooley said. "You tell your mama, Byron."

"Yes, ma'am, I'll tell her."

Naomi squawked as I grabbed her away from the crayons, and she hollered all the way home. I fed her the Gerber's Mama'd left out for me to warm up, gave her a bath, and waited for her to fall asleep.

It was like somebody'd wound her up with a key—gimme this, gimme that, bouncing up and down in her crib when I tried to lay her down. Eight o'clock came, then nine and nine-thirty. I kept looking at Marshalk's, and sure enough the lights went off at nine, like always. But with Naomi still carrying on, Marshalk might not be asleep when we went in.

Then what?

I put on a dark shirt and pants, like Marvin said. I watched the second hand circle the electric clock. I went to the bathroom. I tried to see behind Marshalk's, where I was supposed to meet the guys, but saw nothing even though I knew they were there. Waiting.

Naomi howled in her crib. Finally at five minutes after ten, no less, she shut up and I was out the door and into the alley.

Marvin grabbed me roughly. "Oughta pound you, makin' us wait like that." Artie and Raymo mumbled assent. "You bring the flashlight?"

I showed him I had.

"Then let's go." He made a cup with his hands that I stepped into and hoisted me to the top of the wall. It was slick from dew, and for a minute I thought I was going to slip off, but I managed to steady up and drop feet first to the other side. We'd picked a night when there was no moon, and it took a second to get my bearings. I was in a garden, alongside a big barrel cactus I'd missed by inches. On my left, a path led to a patio and the house. The gate out to the alley was to my right.

I slid the bolt and let Marvin, Artie, and Raymo through.

"Damn it's dark," Raymo said.

"Shut up, fool. Byron, don't use the flash till you're inside. Signal us from the back door, okay?"

"Okay. But watch out for cactus. There's one right—"

"Owww," Artie said. "Son of a—"

"Go, Byron."

I went. The basement window was the key, spotted when the guys were over one day hatching the plan. I eased over there, looking indirectly at it the way I'd learned in scouts before I had to quit because of no money. The window looked small, but that's why I got the job. None of the others would have made it.

It was locked. Just as we expected.

I took out the little glass cutting tool Artie'd shown me how to use and etched a circle around where the latch was. But the little suction thing wasn't wet enough or something, and when I tapped the glass it fell out on the ground and broke.

I froze, expecting a hand to come out and grab me; thank God none did, because I'd have died right there. Finally I started to breathe again, and from the wall I saw the vague outline of Marvin waving me on. Thinking hard about the money, I reached in and found the latch.

After all that it gave easily, the window propped open no problem, and I was inside the basement, trying to see something—anything. Lord, it was dark in there. I flipped on the flash. Boxes were everywhere and there was a taller wardrobe carrier I'd seen the movers hauling in. On shelves were smaller boxes, books, and jars. Across from me, the stairs led to a door.

I crept across the concrete floor and up, wondering what I'd do if the door was locked. So far, so good—it wasn't. I opened it, looked around. The kitchen: sink, stove, and refrigerator to my left; breakfast alcove on the right; large plant, a palm or something, in the corner. Dead ahead was the back door, its window looking out on the patio and garden.

I made my way toward it so I could unlock and signal. Almost home.

"Don't move, please. I have a gun." The voice was taut and lightly accented. It also scared the living hell out of me.

The flash dropped from my hands and rolled away. I was dead—in a dark house with no idea of who or what I was facing. "Gun" rang in my ears. Whoever it was was going to shoot me.

The lights came on and he stepped out from behind the palm.

He wasn't much bigger than I was, five-six or seven if that. He wore a fabric jacket of some kind, its reddish color vivid contrast to the palest face I'd ever seen. He looked bleached. Thin and bleached. Dark eyebrows made it even more pronounced; black eyes bored into, through me, and out the other side. My own eyes were on the small revolver he held in his left hand.

"I assume that clunk we just heard from outside was your friends abandoning you," he said.

I eyed the open door to the cellar, but he reached over and shut it. I'd already seen the bolt and chain on the back door. I looked down at my pants. It was bad.

"Seems you've had an accident," he said calmly, dropping the pistol into his other pocket. "Do you do this kind of thing often?"

I said nothing; what was there to say?

"Answer me, please."

"No," I managed, feeling awful.

"And may I assume your mother doesn't know you're here? Byron Whitaker from next door."

Oh, God, he knew my name. My life was over—Mama'd kill me if he didn't. "No," I said. "I mean yes."

"I see." He thought a moment, the pause letting me see how peaked he really was. The skin of his face was pulled back from prominent cheekbones and teeth that looked too large. I thought about pushing him over and running, but where?

He reached a decision. "I'm prepared to offer you a bargain. I advise you to take it, as I won't offer again."

I looked at him as a drowning man must look at a lifeboat.

"Here it is," he said. "You help me every day after school for a week, and I won't mention this to your mother. Agree and you're free to go. Otherwise..."

"Deal," I squeaked. I couldn't believe it, I was getting out alive.

He picked up my flash and turned on the porch light, illuminating the back yard, wall, and gate. "If I don't see you tomorrow, I will go to your mother with this." He held up the flash. "As for tonight, be thankful you broke into Ludwig Marshalk's house and not someone else's." He slipped the chain off the back door and worked the bolt. "Now get out of here."

I did.

I'd just finished changing, rinsing the rank smell out of my wet pants, when Mama got home. She'd been right: There was a God.

Marvin was mad. I could tell by the way he had my arm bent back.

"Gotta be more to it than that," he said.

"Yeah," Raymo echoed, licking his lips. "Talk, By-ron."

I told them again about the bargain. Finally Marvin let me go, and I rubbed the feeling back into my shoulder.

"Damn, this might be better anyway," Artie said to Marvin, who was thinking hard about this new development. "More time for the punk to find the guy's money. Whole week."

Marvin and Raymo joined Artie in a smile as it dawned on them.

Looking at their faces, I felt like the beef in a roast beef sandwich.

At first we were wary of each other, Ludwig Marshalk and I, but it passed. He seemed to know that I had to mind the baby, and he let me bring her over after Titus was gone—back door, of course, so nobody'd know and mention it to Mama, arouse her suspicions. Even had a little area set up for Naomi and things for her to play with.

The house was way different than ours and not just bigger. It had a sunken living room, tile on the floor, paintings and expensive things on the walls, matching furniture. Money there, all right. The drapes were kept closed as usual, but that was okay, kind of cozy feeling. Helped keep the house warm, he said, and it was—near 80 in there. But I figured that was more for his illness, whatever it was, and after a while I didn't even notice. Actually, he looked better than last time, as if somebody'd put makeup on him, but that couldn't be right since he was a man

Anyway, what he wanted me to do seemed simple enough, just organize his stuff from the basement while he sat in a chair and told me which was what. Clothes, furnishings, things he seemed anxious to get rid of, most of it old, like you'd see in a museum. Some I'd liked to have given Mama, but that would have put her wise. A lot we set out for the trash. Other stuff we set aside with names of people or charities.

Putting it in order, he said. But never more than three hours at a time. You could just see the fatigue draining his enthusiasm. And I never saw him eat.

About the third day I guess it was, Marvin still hounding me about Ludwig Marshalk's money, we hit the boxes of photographs. Piles of them that he wanted put by category into the albums he'd set aside for some library.

I'd seen photographs, even taken some with a Brownie camera of Daddy's before it broke, but I'd never seen anything like these. It was like looking into another place and time: black and white scenes, people in old-looking clothes and hair. Seemed like I asked about every one; it slowed our progress, but I didn't care. Strangely enough, neither did he.

Many were pictures of him as a boy in Romania, where he'd been born. Others were of his wife, darkly pretty even though her clothes were out of date. He didn't say much about her, except that she'd died a long time ago in 1917 of a virus—her and their little boy. The boy was in the pictures, too, different ages up to about mine. A lot of these Mr. Marshalk just shook his head at, as though I wasn't there.

Movie scenes he had a ton of; stills, he called them. Others had actors in poses, with autographs and little notes. Some pretty personal.

"How do you have these?" I asked. "Were you in the movies?"

"Not exactly," he said, running a hand over thinning hair. "I knew someone in silent films."

I'd seen a silent film one Saturday morning at the Leimert Theater, cops racing around or something. Silly without the sound.

"Who are all these addressed to? I-G-O-R..."

"Igor Lantz. You wouldn't know him."

"Why, is he dead?"

"Quite." He rummaged and came up with a scary-looking full-length portrait of a man all in black posed beside a crypt. Shadows obscured most of his face, but the eyes gave me chills. They burned out at the camera as if to say, "No place to hide, sucker. You're mine."

"Was this guy a real vampire or what?"

"No, it was just a part he was known for. Nosferatu."

"Say what?"

He spelled it for me. "You like the movies?" Moovez, it sounded like when he said it, something I was getting used to, like the heat.

"Sure, when I have the money. Who doesn't?"

He reached into his pocket, came out with a five-dollar bill, which he put in my hand. "Go—take a friend. Enjoy yourself."

I was speechless. Here I'd busted into the guy's house, broke his window, was still looking to rob him, and he gives me—

"You earned it, Byron. A man needs to earn his place in the world. Now enough for one day, I'm tired."

So it went through the end of the week, the one right before Christmas vacation started. The one where I was going to take the money I hadn't found yet and go find my father.

We'd finished the photos and were almost through with the last box when I pulled out two things that looked like braces you strapped onto your legs. Like stilts, but shorter.

"Where you want these?" I asked.

He thought, looking tireder than I'd seen him all week. "Over there by the wardrobe. A costume shop might take them."

"You ready to do the wardrobe now?"

He looked at the six-foot-tall carrier tied up with rope. "No. We won't be doing that."

Seemed strange, leaving one undone. "How come?" I asked.

"Just a lot of old dead things. I'll tell Titus—" He sagged in the chair.

"Mr. Marshalk?" I stepped closer, but his eyes had shut and his mouth was open. His breathing sounded heavy, like Mama's when she drifted off on the couch.

My big chance to look for places where he might've hid his cash: closets upstairs that had looked promising, under his mattress, other spots I'd seen when he showed me the house. I raced up the stairs and was about to open the hall closet when something stopped me, I don't know what. Maybe it was the way he looked. Small and helpless.

I got a glass of water from the kitchen and went back down.

He wasn't in the chair. Prickles shot up and down my back.

"Is that for me?" He was leaning against the far wall by the broken window, sucking in fresh air. He held out a bony arm. I brought him the water, my eyes still wide.

"Sorry to frighten you," he said after downing some. "I thought you were upstairs going—gone, I mean."

"What happened to you, passin' out like that?"

"Just a little problem I have. Goes with getting old." He took his hand off the wall, stood, tottered, steadied.

"Are you okay?"

"Take tonight off, Byron, and we'll finish up Saturday. That should do it."

I helped him up the stairs and left, wondering what really happened down there.

Saturday afternoon, Marvin found the five bucks.

"Big money for such a little guy, don't you think?" he said going through my jacket. His eyes got hard and mean. "Your Mama didn't give you no five bucks, that's for sure."

I watched his fist swing lazily up, and the next thing I knew I was in the dirt, my nose bleeding and Marvin right over me. "That's a sample of what we give guys who hold out on us," he said, the cigarette dangling from his mouth.

Raymo pressed the switch on his knife and the blade flicked out. He handed it to Marvin, who held it at my neck. "The only reason I don't cut your head off right now is because you know where things are in that house. Now I'm tired of waiting. Be in the alley tonight, 'cause we're going in. All of us."

He drew the blade lightly across my throat.

"Old man Marshalk better not give us no trouble either."

Mama left for work at four, checking my puffed nose before she left. Kickball in the face, I told her, had to happen sometime.

"Never seen you take one on the nose before, Byron. You been brawlin'?"

"No ma'am," I lied. Wasn't a lie, actually. Brawling takes two, and I wasn't stupid enough to take a swing at Marvin. "Have a good shift," I said as she went out the door.

For some reason I felt a lump in my throat when she left. Probably the bop I took. Naomi was still fussy from her cold, but unlike Monday she dropped off to sleep at seven, which was good because I wasn't about to take her to Marshalk's with me. One Whitaker in danger was enough, thank you.

"Whatever happened with those boys, Byron, the ones who took off on you?" We were just finishing up, marking some last items for Mr. Titus to dispose of, when he asked. Maybe he'd seen how distracted I was, what with Marvin, Artie, and Raymo likely outside the wall right now, and me wondering what the hell I was going to do about it.

"Oh, I don't know," I said. "They're around."

"It's always harder to do the right thing," he said after a bit. "Especially when the rest of the world is bigger than you are. Believe me, I know."

I didn't say anything, just felt small.

"There'll always be bullies. And not enough people to stand up to them. It's what they feed on, like vampires."

We went upstairs then, and suddenly the house felt very hot. I wiped my forehead while Ludwig Marshalk went to get something from his bedroom. I checked the little mantle clock: almost ten.

I was thinking of telling him the whole thing when he emerged from the hallway. In his hand was a squarish flat package, which he gave me.

"What is it?" I asked dumbly.

"You've never seen a Christmas present before?"

"But I don't have anything for you."

"The basement, that's my present. Now I can—prepare." His eyes looked especially bright and there was a flush on his neck.

"Prepare for what?"

"Nothing. Come over by the window. He surprised me by turning off the light. "Look up there. See that one just to the left of the Pleiades?"

"The what?"

"Those stars there. That one to the left."

Naturally, I thought this was odd. "So?" I said, spotting it, thinking his condition had caught up with his brain.

"Somebody gave it to me a long time ago. It's a lucky star. Now I'm giving it to you."

What do you say to that? I looked at it, then at him, back at it.

"Talk to it, give it a name. Or don't if you can't. But that would be a shame, because it works."

"Then why you giving it away?"

"Because it's time. And speaking of that, I think you had better go. Merry Christmas, Byron," he said quietly. "We're finished here."

When I closed the gate, it was as if I'd stepped into a horror film. Marshalk had killed his lights when I left, so the alley was all shadows. Branches hung down and strewn junk made eerie shapes. Even worse, mist had started to gather— damp as a wet sheet and smelling like one, dripping off the leaves. I tried to find the star, but couldn't through the trees.

Maybe they weren't waiting there, maybe they hadn't—

Marvin grabbed my arm, scaring the crap out of me.

"There is no money, Marvin," I yelped. "We were wrong."

"What'd I tell you," Artie said. "The little shit's cut us out."

"Guess so," Marvin said. "And after everything we told him, too."

The first blow knocked the breath out of me, the next whanged off my ear. I staggered, gasping, and the next one put me down. They were on me then, hitting me while I tried to roll myself into a ball. Finally Marvin, I guess it was, yanked me to my feet and drove a fist into my face. On my knees, I gagged, spat broken teeth and blood. A final kick bounced me off Marshalk's wall and into semi-consciousness.

From far off, I heard the click of the switchblade and Raymo saying, "Yeah, do it, Marvin. Then the old man."

I managed to look Marvin in the face and blubber something about not hurting Mr. Marshalk, that he was sick, then I heard the gate swing open behind us and Marvin's eyes rose from me and got huge. "Sweet Jesus," he said. "What is that?"

Artie made a strangled sound beside him and fell back. Somebody moaned, Raymo I think.

Still dazed, I managed to look behind me. The thing was at least seven feet tall, all in black and caped. Its head was bald and skull-like, its ears pointed, the eyes huge and terrifying. Slowly it revealed fangs that were red with blood. Then it raised one talon-like finger at Marvin.

"Oh God, please, no," he croaked.

That's when I passed out.

I have no idea how, but I was on the couch when Mama came home from work, took one look at my face and screamed bloody murder. Finally I got her calmed down. But I had to tell her about Marvin, Artie, and Raymo beating on me for some money I earned from Mr. Marshalk. Trying to get enough to buy her a Christmas present is how I put it, my fingers crossed behind my back.

She burst into tears then and held me, but I was glad when I finally got to bed, the aspirin she'd given me making me feel a little better.

Next day she went after my attackers.

Artie's and Raymo's parents were alternately apologetic to her and mad at them, she said, and they must have come down hard because I had no further trouble with either of them. Raymo avoided me altogether at school. Artie stuck close to Crenshaw.

As for Marvin, we heard he went to live with a cousin out of state. Which apparently was more or less okay with Marvin's mother and the eight other kids in the Hall family. Guess Marvin wasn't too popular there, either.

Ludwig Marshalk and I never spoke again. Two days before Christmas, we had a visit from Mr. Titus, who told us our neighbor had died of advanced pernicious anemia, a rare blood disorder that made him so weak his heart stopped.

"The poor man," Mama said.

"Yeah, he really went downhill after the weekend," Titus said. "Couldn't even lift his head."

Mama went in the kitchen to get Titus some tea and homemade cookies. After she'd gone, Titus handed me a package from under his coat. Dirt was on the wrapping and one corner had a rip, but I recognized it right away. He said, "This was on Mr. Marshalk's desk with a note to give it to you personally and confidentially. Said you'd dropped it." He looked at me as though expecting I'd tell him all about it, man to man or something.

"Thanks, Mr. Titus," I said. Then I went to my room.

Of course it was the picture of Nosferatu. But what made me sad, opening it in my room on Christmas morning in 1953 before Mama and Naomi were even out of bed, the house all quiet, was the writing he'd put on it: To Byron, who proved to be very tall indeed. From your friend, Ludwig Marshalk (Igor Lantz).

I hoped my tears wouldn't lower me in his eyes if he happened to be watching.

Jingle Bells coming from somewhere snapped me out of it. I took a last drag on the cigarette, crushed it in the ashtray, craned my head out the car window. It was quite dark now and cool, and mist was starting to rise off the damp lawns and gather in the low spots.

And there it was—the lucky star he'd given me so long ago.

Did it work as he said? Not with my dad when we finally did get together. But then maybe his new wife and situation had more to do with that, her having three kids and all. At any rate, it helped Mama over some rough spots, and even though I couldn't see it in Vietnam, I felt it up there, keeping me in one piece when I was so scared I couldn't get my breath. My fellow sufferers in the acting profession might consider two academy award nominations a pretty fair track record, too. See, Marshalk gave me that as well. I mean if I didn't know what an academy award performance was after seeing him in action, who did?

I cast a final look upward, smiled at Ludwig and turned the key. Driving away, I made a mental note to call the realtor whose phone number was on that sign.

Just for luck, you understand.

Foreword to
The Gift

Gary Phillips

There's a power in fables that pulls at us, that springs from stories told around the fires when our ancestors looked up at the starry night and wondered if there were more. Not necessarily were they contemplating that something beyond the sky, as Sam Cooke alluded to, but what our place was in the big scheme of a too-often-hostile universe. What besides an opposable thumb made us different than the other animals clawing and scratching through life?

Certainly, in Richard Barre's *The Gift,* Eddie Dockweiler, his main character in the tale, is clawing and scratching to maintain his hand-to-mouth existence in a wintery New York City. It's hard to imagine that Eddie, like a battered, discarded car spied on an empty lot, once rolled new and shiny. He was not always a wreck, panhandling for food and rent. He was once a teenaged soldier in the Korean War, referred to in history as the Forgotten War. But Eddie hasn't forgotten Korea and the cost paid by his buddy; how that incident and other events have affected him has led to where we come upon him.

For it is Christmastime in the freezing Big Apple and Eddie has a dream of making it out to the other coast to be a beach bum—if only a certain large individual with a crappy attitude wouldn't keep jacking his hard-begged-for money. But the strong-arm specialist isn't Eddie's only concern, and the heart of the story, riffing as it does, just a bit, on the cold-eyed romanticism of Damon Runyon, plays out deftly under Barre's practiced storytelling.

Though life has long since forgotten Eddie, in *The Gift* he proves you can't give up on yourself or others. Come along those cracked sidewalks and bleak alleyways and see for yourself.

The Gift

Eddie Dockweiler had no idea where the cab came from—the one that nearly knocked him across Fifth Avenue and into the next world—just that it scared the living crap out of him. Which didn't for a second stop him from reacting the way any red-blooded New Yorker would.

"Moron! Whaddaya, blind? I'm walkin' here." Blowing enough steam into the twenty-degree air to resemble one of the underground vents. Beating a tattoo with his fists on the icy yellow hood.

The cab driver, though impossible for him to look pale under his turban, at least *appeared* shaken. Which didn't stop him from suggesting that Eddie kiss the business end of his tail pipe before speeding down 50th Street with a bump that drew sparks from his undercarriage. Giving, in Eddie's mind, new meaning to the term "bat out of hell."

He raised a one-finger salute at the retreating Caprice. *"And the camel you rode in on!"*

Christmas shoppers streaming out of Rockefeller Plaza and around him took their usual notice of such things. None.

What had really set Eddie off, of course, made him oblivious to the bat out of hell, was the sight of Neigh-Neigh appropriating his primo spot next to the right-side bronze door of Saint Patrick's Cathedral.

All he needed right now.

Sure, it might have served him right for warming up a little longer in the Public Library. But this was too much. Even for a forgiving type like himself.

Neigh-Neigh saw him coming—scurrying might be a better term for a man of his size—up the granite steps, the church itself with its buttresses, towers, and spires looking like some frosted Christmas confection. Even though the storm had abated long enough to cast down a timid sun.

"Eddie..."

"You're in my spot."

"Keepin' it warm, that's all. Savin' it for you." Her breath plumed in the wind off the river, and her nose was pink from the cold.

"Move it, Neigh."

"Just had it in mind to wish you a Merry Christmas, Eddie. Merry Christmas."

"Lot merrier when you're outta my spot."

"Kind of greeting is that for a friend?"

"Christmas ain't for two days yet, and you're costing me money. Now move."

"It was just in case I didn't see you later."

"Which you won't if I can help it, Neigh. Now I'm telling you—"

"How hard is it to call a girl by her right name?"

Eddie did a mock look-around. "Girl? What girl? Anybody see a girl here?" Shoveling on the amazement as if he had an audience. "All I see is a horse."

She didn't look like one, of course. Penny'd given her the handle because of that ugly blankety thing she always wore. Right out of some stable. Actually, she wasn't bad looking if you squinted around the gin blossoms. A bit like Claudette Colbert, that same wide-eyed resilience. Nothing he'd ever tell her. All he needed was somebody named Nalene Birdsell from South Dakota hanging around his neck. Like the one time when they'd bottomed out on muscatel entitled her to permanent dibseys on him or something.

Jeez...

Flush-looking prospects were going in and out of the Cathedral interior aglow with holiday candles and goodwill—*his* goodwill. But who knew? You had to make eye contact—with them, not with Neigh-Neigh standing here giving him grief.

She was opening her mouth to respond, when he kind-of-sort-of gave her this little bump. Encouragement was all it was, really. Hardly anything that would cause a person to lose her balance.

Certainly nothing to make her roll all the way to the sidewalk.

Lord, Lord, Eddie thought, taking the steps two at a time. Kneeling beside her as the foot traffic began to part around her.

"Damn, Neigh. You all right?" Eddie asked as she looked up at him. Didn't appear serious, no blood or anything.

"No thanks to you, Eddie Dockweiler." She got gingerly to her feet.

Brushing slush and gum wrappers off her shock-absorbing blanket-coat, Eddie felt an emotion akin to relief. Nothing broken. Couldn't be too careful these days, what with all the friggin' lawyers ready to sue your pants off. He had a brief flash on what it would be like without pants in this weather, so far the coldest on record or some such. *California here I come....*

"No thanks to you at all."

"Come on, Neigh. Not my fault you can't stand up." Ten in the morning, for crying out loud. "How much you put away already?"

"Nothing—yet," she said in that dignity-saving tone of hers; the queen of Siam when she got it in her head. "So long, Eddie. I'd stick around, but I might freeze to death. And I'm not talking about the weather."

After an unsteady half-block, she was swallowed by the glut of people waiting to cross at 51st. Eddie glanced around to see if there were disapproving stares, of course seeing none, then mounted the steps and took his place at the right hand of God. Just as the bells of St. Patrick's broke into *Adeste Fidelis.*

By Angelus, Eddie had exactly twenty-two dollars and eighteen cents, the cents coming from a wasp-looking kid whose parents had chatted-up and sent over. Two from the parents, eighteen cents from the kid.

"God bless you," he'd said, his standard reply—thinking, *Try it some time. Let's see you look deserving for eight hours.*

And yet he knew his role in where and what he was. A weakness for sour mash whiskey and an inexhaustible distaste for work that had combined to narrow his career path somewhat.

Screw it, he thought. No sense reliving all that.

Eddie shivered in a gust that felt like more sleet. Clutching his overcoat at the neck, he couldn't resist a glance inside the Cathedral—at the grandeur, the people alone and in groups. Some knelt in prayer, others craned their necks at the vaulted stonework and stained glass, others strolled around as if it were Churchworld or something. But whatever moved them, whatever they felt coming out, Eddie was waiting to help with the transition—fingerless-gloved hand at just the right angle to his diminutive frame.

Paper covers stone; donation covers guilt. Everybody wins.

Another strong gust felt like a hand trying to nudge him in, but Eddie was having none of that. Way too late to make amends now. He'd given You-Know-Who plenty of opportunity while he was in free fall. Bargaining in the night; tears and promises and carrying on. There'd be no kissing and making up now.

Besides, in a week he'd be in L.A., warming his toes in the sunshine. Living off the fat of the land. Few more good days, that's all it would take. Then—outta here.

Pretending he was hiking up his trousers, he felt the moneybelt around his middle. Four-forty and change, sixty to go—like money in the bank, only better. His ticket to ride.

Singing "I Love New York," substituting "Hate" for "Love," Eddie turned his face to the wind and danced down the steps.

Warmer from the forty-block trek and various pre-owned edibles appropriated along the way, Eddie was almost to his flop when he saw Hurley coming out of the alley beside it. Heading straight for him.

Damn.

"Yo, runt. We needs to talk."

Eddie felt himself being dragged into the alley, Hurley bigger by a good foot and at least a hundred pounds. Ex-football player, Penny had told him; good dude to stay clear of on any given day. Injuries that no amount of painkillers could reach had only added to the mean streak.

"Now, then..."

"Hurley...just thinkin'a you."

"Uh-huh. What'd we score today, m'man?"

We. "Nothing much—few bucks." He felt the twenty-two and change in his coat pocket, wished to hell he'd belted the L.A. half like he'd planned before it got so cold.

Hurley wiped his nose on the sleeve of his parka, leaving a silvery path that reminded Eddie of a snail's across a wet lawn. His leer showcased bad teeth, one porcelain incisor the white oddity in his full-moon face.

"Friggin' weather. Nobody feelin'—"

The blow came with Eddie's hand still in his coat pocket, even though he'd been prepared to dodge and yell. Not that it would have done him much good in that neighborhood—flophouses and flop people the big man preyed on to score cash for the skag that kept him marginal.

But doubled over now, Eddie had other things to worry about. Breathing, for instance. Fighting for air as Hurley yanked the bills out of his pocket, bouncing the kid's eighteen cents off a dumpster with a sound like shotgun pellets.

For a moment, Eddie was panicked Hurley would rip him apart, find the money belt and that would be it. But that would have taken some doing dressed as he was in thermals, two sweatshirts, two pairs of pants, wool sport coat and muffler, the overcoat, a flapped hat. Besides, it was heading toward zero now, and putting himself in Hurley's place, twenty-two wasn't bad for a few minutes' work.

Hurley moved to the mouth of the alley. There he seemed to have a change of heart, and Eddie saw him coming back.

God, not the belt!

Eddie wasn't much quicker dodging the kick, but at least he'd altered its angle by the time it knocked his hat off. He heard, "Know you got more somewhere. That's for next time." Then he was drifting, and a light snow was falling on him. Just like Korea—dug in on this godforsaken ridge in the worst cold he'd ever experienced. Seventeen and just out of high school, his father more than willing to sign the papers.

Artie Markham had shared his foxhole—same age he was, a pal since boot. And by the time the firing had stopped and his hands were up, squint dead everywhere you looked, some right up to their berm, snowmelt hissing on their overheated and jammed rifles, cranberry sauce was all Artie'd had left for a head.

Eddie saw himself stumbling from the foxhole, the faces of his captors. Suddenly he was awake and jerking back against the alley wall. This was no dream, and the faces were closing in....

Eddie got a grip, realized it was a man, a woman, and a kid about a year old in her arms. Staring down at him.

"Jesus, Mary and Joseph," he said. "Don't friggin' *do* that to me." He pressed against the brick until he was almost upright, saw the man and woman were about the same height he was, maybe a little smaller.

"Coulda killed you."

They looked at him with solemn faces.

"War—I was in a war. Killed people looked like you."

Their eyes widened, and they glanced at each other.

Eddie got it: language barrier. "Slopes, squints, slants," he added.

The man nodded, crossed his arms across the vinyl jacket he wore over a thin white shirt and too-loose plaid pants.

A caution light flashed in Eddie's head. "You *don't* speak English, do you?"

"Eng...rish," the man echoed.

"Same to you." Smiling as he said it.

The woman smiled back, or tried to, cold as she must have been in her cotton sundress and quilted navy raincoat—even the baby's breath showing from the blue blanket she had him wrapped in.

"Shipjumpers," Eddie said. "Perfect." Feeling more like himself now, his wind back and the money belt undisturbed. Still, he was out the twenty-two—which meant tapping the stash to pay tonight's eight-buck, highway-robbery rack rate, maybe a short-dog of antifreeze. Plus, despite the padding, his ribs were starting to hurt where Hurley'd nailed him.

The man put out a hand to steady him.

Eddie brushed it aside. "Stand back. Pfc. Eddie Dockweiler coming through." He straightened, brushed snow and alley from his overcoat.

"*Ed..dee,*" he heard the woman say as he turned the corner.

Eddie looked himself in the mirror, turned away from the extended forehead and grizzled face staring back at him. Bald he could handle; it was the grizzled that got to him. His father had been grizzled. Like the man's bony finger was pointing from the grave, decreeing that his son be grizzled as well.

Stay tuned, Eddie thought. *Beach bum coming up.*

But not unless he got a good deal better at avoiding Hurley. He made a mental note to be more alert, then tried mouthwashing out whatever it was he polished off last night. Polish—not a happy thought.

He downed the rest of the mouthwash.

He was bundled-up and downstairs, passing the front desk and the slant manager of the place, asshole Lumm, browbeating a hunched-over denizen, when he saw them. Coming out of the alley. Shaking a gray blanket the man was trying to fold in the wind—without much success, Eddie noted. Until the woman put the baby down and took the other end, the baby setting up a wail that went right through Eddie's tender cortex.

As he stepped outside, the woman got the blanket folded, the baby quieted. The man spotted him and moved closer.

"*Ed...dee,*" he said, bowing. "*Eng..rish.*"

"*Jeez,*" Eddie marveled. "You spent last night in the alley?" Four below, somebody in the hallway'd muttered to him on the way down.

The woman looked as if she were struggling with something. She made a circle with her thumb and index finger, looked at the man for confirmation. "*You...OK?*"

That was when Eddie headed up the block.

* * *

After a wash in the Lib, hot water a dead issue in his fleabag room, Eddie was ready as he'd ever be. One bag of discard doughnuts later, he was back at his post in front of Saint Pat's.

Red-cheeked visitors, moved by Eddie's practiced look and the wind tugging at his coat, were feeling generous this morning, and his spirits lifted beyond the humiliation of last night. Friggin' Hurley—maybe he'd kill the guy after all. Find out where he slept and garrotte him or something.

Yeah, right.

Lunchtime came and went, Eddie leaning against the Cathedral as though faint from hunger, while in fact taking count. Twenty bucks—on a roll. Then the weather closed in, the wind got mean, and the supply of faithful dropped with the temperature.

Thinking of palm trees, Eddie stuck it out. It was either that or—

Three faces looked up at him from the sidewalk.

No! *No, no, no....*

Eddie snapped a *getoutahere* gesture at them, nearly striking a woman approaching with a rolled-up bill in her hand. As she hurried away, he swore, causing her to look back.

"No," he said quickly. "Not you—*them.*"

"Shame on you," she hissed at him.

Eddie gritted his teeth. Glancing around first for Neigh-Neigh or some other opportunist who might have designs on his post, he left it and fronted the three.

"Go away," he said into the teeth of the wind. *"I'm workin'."*

They looked at him; this close, Eddie could see them shivering in their mismatched clothing. *Just like at Pyongyang,* he thought—whole families looking stone-faced as his line of POWs passed by.

Bullshit—this had to stop. "Get outta here!" he yelled.

Nothing.

"You can't stay here."

Not a movement.

Finally he reached out and shoved the man, who slipped on the icy sidewalk and...just stayed there...looking at Eddie. All of them—looking at him. Not saying anything.

Cursing under his breath, Eddie trudged back up to his post, willing himself not to acknowledge them with even a look. Finally, after what seemed like a half-hour, he swung a peek down the steps, noting with relief they were gone.

Neigh-Neigh left a spot she was working down by Grand Central Station, caught up with him as he was waiting for WALK.

"Hi Eddie. Got enough to go to California yet?"

"Who told you about that? Friggin' Penny, I suppose."

She winked at him coyly. "I remember who did...and when."

"You wish."

The light changed and he darted across Madison Avenue toward the Library. But she darted right alongside.

"Take me with you," she said.

"You gotta be kidding."

"You said you loved me."

"People say a lot of things. Doesn't mean they mean them. Besides, you're younger than me."

"A few years, big deal."

"Try twenty."

"What's that when you love somebody? You've got a heart, Eddie, I know you do. You just have to let it out once in a while." She nearly bumped into a tall man with a briefcase, but she kept up as Eddie edged around a group of nuns.

"We could make a new start."

"Yeah? Then what?"

"Be together—what else?"

Eddie looked at her. For a moment he was swayed by the longing in her voice, the lit-up shop windows with the schmaltzy music blaring out, the shoppers buying things for other people. The promise of it all. Then the light changed and he realized her longing was likely more for anyplace other than here, this shit weather. It had nothing to do with him. She'd just leave him like everybody else in his life had. Probably even before he left her.

The spell broken, Eddie created a pick around a red-suited Santa weaving up 42nd and bolted for the Lib.

Eddie sank deeper into his overcoat, edged around the corner. Good—Hurley was nowhere around. *Probably lying in an alley with a knife in his throat*, he thought—what he deserved. Picking on somebody who could fight back.

However momentarily, the stars were out now, the temperature already feeling colder than last night. He was almost to the flop's fire door, still watching out for Hurley, figuring it was probably too cold even for him, when he heard them.

Felt them, actually.

"Ed...dee," the woman said softly.

"Jesus, Mary and Joseph," he said as they stepped from the dark of the alley and into the light. For a moment they all just stood there. Then Eddie heard someone saying in a voice that sounded like but he knew couldn't be his, *"What the Sam Hill am I going to do with you?"*

"Jesus...Mary...Joseph," he said pointing to each in turn. "If I gotta call you something, might as well be that." *Lord,* he thought, *what would Artie think?* Probably get a howl out of it, knowing him. Funny how he could still recall the kid's Okie laugh, high-pitched and all-embracing, even under the worst conditions.

Like now.

They were in his room—actually in his room—snuck up the fire stairs or Mr. Lumm would have thrown all four of them out in a New York minute—cold or no. At least here the temperature hovered above freezing, depending on how stoned the guy in the basement was.

As they watched Jesus crawling around on the sprung bed, the woman having made short work of the room, tidying it as best she could, Eddie felt oddly embarrassed at how shabby the place was. Lath where plaster should have been, everything smelling bad from the decades of burst pipes and backed-up drains—his share among them, he thought sheepishly. He sat in the lone chair while the man braced himself against the sink with the HOT tap that didn't work.

"So. Where you from?"

They smiled at him.

"China? Korea? Outer Mongolia?"

Smiling and nodding.

Like waking up in 1952. "How?" he asked. As they looked at each other, he made a boat with his hand, bobbing on waves. "Boat?"

They nodded. Smiled.

Great.

Eddie said, "Tomorrow—you go away." He attempted sign language to get the point across, though he knew it was futile. If it didn't work out there, what made him think it would work in here?

Sure enough, Joseph and Mary just smiled and nodded. That's when Eddie decided on a different tack: See how long their smiles and nods would last in the face of his life story.

Three hours later he'd covered his old man, the suicide of his mother, where his brother theoretically had gone because nobody in the family knew and besides they were all dead now, Korea—along with some unaccustomed welling up when he told them about Artie Markham, Mary and Joseph's expressions becoming grave right along with his.

Mary rocked Jesus now, the kid's dark eyes fixed on Eddie as if he could see inside him. Disconcerting until Eddie realized he was just staring the way kids that age did.

Picking it up again, Eddie covered his brief career in sales, two ex-wives taking him to the cleaners, winding up on the streets, what that was like, his plan to go to California.

"Almost got the money raised. Right here."

Nods all around as Eddie patted his belt. It was almost fun, he thought—no lip to worry about, no interruptions or judging. Like it didn't hurt to open up. He decided to branch out.

"This dame I know—girl, I mean—younger than me. She wants to come along. I mean, she can't—what would I do with her? Nice enough, I suppose, but can you see me with...no, of course you can't. Not even my friend Penny could. And neither can I. Besides, Neigh—Nalene, her name is—she could do a whole lot better, she just doesn't know it. Cut out the gin, find the right guy...outta here. Now me—"

Suddenly it struck Eddie that everything he was going to say about himself was so much bull.

He decided they'd had about enough for one night.

Eddie lay awake a long time after they'd tried to make themselves comfortable—him on the box spring, Mary and Jesus on the mattress, Joseph wedged in the corner. Still, in a strange way, their breathing and little sleep noises were comforting, and when he woke up later than usual and they were gone, he almost missed them.

He was dressed and easing through the flop's lifeless lobby when Mr. Lumm spotted him, called him over. Wondering what the asshole wanted, Eddie shrugged and went.

"You have *people* in your room."

Somebody'd squealed, Eddie realized; probably for a break on the rate. "Relatives," he bluffed.

"No, no, no. Boat people. I see them." He pointed to the wall where a sheet of paper was tacked. "Owe me twenty-fye dollars."

"No way."

"Twenty-fye now, or I call cops."

Eddie broke off, went back up to his room, where he withdrew a twenty and a five from the belt. Cursing louder at each floor, he hit the lobby and handed Lumm the bills—which Mr. Lumm then slipped into his pocket.

"Against house rules," he said. "Once okay since you stay here before. Happen again, I throw *you* out. Understand?"

"Merry Christmas Eve to you, too, Lumm."

"Like you always tell *me*. Throw the bums out."

"I.... They're not bums, they're cold and—"

"Yeah, yeah, yeah. What you think this place is, Erris Eyrand?" Mr. Lumm turned back to his desk work.

Making matters worse, Jesus, Mary and Joseph were waiting for him near the alley.

"Jerks almost got me thrown out," he greeted them with. *"Go away."* His breath fogging in the cold air. At least it wasn't snowing—yet.

They responded by nodding; then to make him feel bad— he just knew because he was on to *their* game—they smiled and bowed.

Eddie responded by cursing and storming up the block. Two blocks, three, four. Pulling away because of Mary's load, but what the hell, an advantage was an advantage, and besides, desperate measures were needed if he was going to make it through this. Besides, Lumm was right—*Throw the bums out* was exactly what he'd said. With every flop in the city SRO in weather like this, he for damned sure wasn't going to get tossed into the street because of some....

Looking back and not seeing them, he decided on a shortcut he knew, put the capper on it. He was halfway through when a familiar shape loomed.

"Well, well. Just who'm lookin' for."

Eddie jumped a mile. *God—not this, too,* ran through his mind. *It's almost your son's birthday, for Christ's sake.*

"Hurley, look. I ain't even had a chance to—"

"Liar. I know about the belt. Had to beat it out of Penny, who by the way ain't feelin' so good right now. Maybe Easter he'll be risin' again." Hurley laughed evilly.

Aw, no...

"Give it up, runt. Before I take everything, leave you to freeze...."

Eddie sagged against the alley wall, his legs jelly as Hurley balled a mammoth fist and cocked it back.

"Ed...dee," a voice called.

And there they were, hustling down the alley toward him. Pink-cheeked from the effort....

Oh, Lord—not them on his conscience, too. Penny was bad enough. "No—get out of here," he shouted. "Run!"

Hurley said, "What's this, your guardian angels? I hate guardian angels."

"You can have the money. Just don't hurt 'em."

"Yeah? Watch this...." Hurley spun away from Eddie and whistled a screamer hook at Joseph.

Except Joseph wasn't there anymore; he was a couple of steps from where he'd been. Eddie wasn't sure he'd seen that right, and Hurley definitely seemed surprised. This time he tried a spin kick that looked to Eddie like it might put a hole in the building, not to mention knock Joseph's block off.

But then Hurley was flying backwards, lifted off his feet as if Joseph had somehow caught his steel-toed boot in midair, twisted it, and flipped him.

Hurley got up slow, raised a hand like he'd had enough, then charged, head down as though bullrushing an opposing lineman. Except it was the dumpster he hit. And this time he stayed down.

For a brief instant Eddie wondered if Hurley were dead— how he looked, anyway—not moving and blood streaming down his face. He cast a mini-glance at the smiling nodding Joseph, who, like a clever bullfighter, somehow had sidestepped Hurley. Or something...Eddie sure didn't know what.

Being the smart operator that he was, however, Eddie Dockweiler beat feet, not stopping to look behind him until he was well within the shadow of the Empire State building.

It was three before Eddie even felt the cold, so wired was he from the run and what had happened. God, what next? Looking around for the three faces he just knew would appear at any second, maybe with the cops in tow. Start pointing at him, for all he knew.

So far, so good, though.

Must be the Christmas Eve traffic, Fifth Avenue full to the curbs with all manner of honking vehicles—looking more like the crawl on 50th and 51st. Every street he could see, for that matter.

Even though the stream of people into the Cathedral was light, the donations he got weren't bad. Only fewer. Or perhaps Eddie's disheveled look said more about that, people giving him a wider berth than usual.

Around dark, snow flurries began and Eddie packed it in. Not knowing what to do, he walked for a couple of hours—Rockefeller Center and the ice skaters, Times Square flashing itself like some futuristic hooker, the Chrysler Building and a hundred more lit up, late shoppers chattering and jamming. The whole city getting ready to heave a collective sigh on Christmas—just another day at the office for Eddie.

As he walked, snow spun down through the lights, softening them and adding that unique crunch to the footfalls. Sounds that recalled trying to catch up to his dad as they left the woods with the fir tree they'd cut down. It was then that Eddie came to terms with what had been bothering him.

Jesus, Mary and Joseph.

Leaving Grand Central Station where he'd taken a moment to freshen up, Eddie headed south toward the flop districts. Thinking even though the temperature had risen a bit with the snow, this was no night to be sleeping on pavement. With a kid. In this town. And screw Lumm—if he found them, they were coming up. After what Joseph did today, he might even pass around a bottle of dirty bird or something. The least he could do.

But where the hell were they?

Eddie felt worse with each passing hour.

Finally he had to score some food, but that wasn't hard when you knew the ropes. Hell, this trio knew from nothing already. *Ed-dee. Eng-lish.* God—what brought them here, anyway? A man'd have to be crazy to expose his family to all this. And what about a mother who'd expose her baby to a bum like Eddie Dockweiler.

Totally beyond him.

Two A.M., his search in high gear. Teeth of the storm now, snow beginning to drift and pile, the trucks already out. Keeping warm by keeping on. Eddie even went back looking for Hurley, but he saw nothing, no stretched-out form. At least it was something. Being linked to a killing—that was *all* he needed.

There he went again, thinking only of himself. He made up for it by redoubling his efforts, looking everywhere he could think of, asking everybody he saw if they'd seen them. Nooks and crannies, cardboard shelters, heater grates, fire barrels with hands extended for warmth. Anything—and nothing.

Like they'd vanished.

Exhausted, he spent the dawn hour in a too-bright doughnut joint. Sitting there in the greasy warmth eating his day-olds, fatigue became guilt, guilt became depression. He'd abandoned them to whatever, and now he had to live with that. Picturing them now, saying their names in his mind, he realized it was Christmas. Merry Christmas, he wished them. Also Penny whom he needed to find and apologize to, himself, Neigh-Neigh, and poor Artie Markham.

Doing the same to the guys making doughnuts, he rebundled and walked outside. Distracted as he was, it was still a beautiful morning: crystalline air he breathed deeply, plumes rising into the sunlight now, finding prisms everywhere he looked. The city at peace for a change.

Nothing left to do, he went back to his room and caught a few hours sack time, then treated himself to a cab, getting to St. Pat's in time for the ten o'clock. Taking up his position, people with happy looks passing by, snow making sculptures of the bare trees on Fifth, breathtaking sounds coming from the organ and bells, he thought maybe there was hope after all. Maybe that's all there was. Just a matter of seeing it.

Then he saw them. Kitty-corner across the Avenue— standing there looking at him.

Eddie knew what he had to do.

Timing a break in the much-lighter Christmas morning traffic, he ran up to them, put an awkward arm around each, touched the baby's face. And then, in full view of God and everybody, he took off his moneybelt, rolled it up, and tucked it inside Mary's coat.

"For the baby," he said. "Merry Christmas from Eddie Dockweiler."

Jesus, Mary and Joseph just looked at him. Then all three smiled. *"Ed-dee,"* they all said. Or so it sounded.

Eddie smiled back, turned toward the Cathedral—where he saw Neigh-Neigh waving to him from his spot. For some reason that didn't bother him either. He just wanted to tell her it was okay, they'd be working the same side of the street now.

Must be the lack of sleep, he thought, timing a return break across Fifth, his heart pounding from the sprint. Not yet sure how he was going to tell her it would be awhile before they saw California.

But then, maybe it didn't matter.

One crossing left—51st—couple of trucks going by. Eddie glanced back to wave again at the three...sunlight bouncing off the Rockefeller building made it impossible to see them. Even shading his eyes, he couldn't. Well, what the heck, they'd be okay now. He was pretty sure of that.

Blinking in the brightness, catching sight of Nalene— *Gonna have to be careful*, he thought, *no more Neigh-Neigh*—Eddie made a run for it.

He had no idea where the cab came from....

Foreword to
Bethany

Robert Crais

Flip a switch, and life snaps into focus. The switch could be anything: a cancer scare, the way light catches in the spring-green leaves, those first crispy wrinkles that appear around your eyes, or a traffic accident in the middle of nowhere late on a frozen night.

Flip a switch, and suddenly the review of a life can be reduced to chilling absolutes: good or hopeless, rich or wasted, worthy or lost. No one judges us more harshly than we judge ourselves, and we are never more merciless with these self-assessments than when we are weak. In these times we see ourselves in the darkest light, without middle ground, and the reviews with which we damn ourselves can contain descriptives such as "failure" and "loser."

The switch is flipped, and we can spiral into hopelessness, seeing only our losses but never our gains.

But by the flip of that same switch...maybe we have a chance to see everything that is good in us and, in that moment, have one final chance at redemption.

No one has done this better—in any form—than Rod Serling. I loved that show—Rod Serling's *The Twilight Zone*—where week after week, Serling offered up stylish, heart-breaking examinations of traveling salesmen, bookish nerds, retirement-home foundlings, and other lost souls staring down the barrels of their own lost lives. Serling delivered these dramas with poignancy and insight, and the poetry of a talent who sensed, innately, that everyone carries within themselves a core of "good" worth saving.

Bethany is such a story.

Richard Barre shows the same depth and humanity that illuminated Serling's work by reminding us—as we question ourselves in bleak moments—of the questions we often forget to ask: Are the switches flipped by chance or design? Are we being given a curse or a gift? A chance not to see weakness, but an opportunity to affirm strength? And if a switch has indeed been switched...by whom?

Bethany

Frank Shane never saw the ice.

He was making good time, no problem there: Oregon border and Mount Shasta back of him, eighty miles to Lakehead and the dam, load of Christmas trees from up near the Idaho border behaving itself behind him.

So far, so good.

Mind over matter.

Old growth closed in around a whitened cut in the hill, retreated behind a fringe of rock-crush, then dropped off to white before shadowing up the other side. Even in storm it was nice country: clean and wooded *before* descending to the farms and valley sprawl, Big-Macs, off-brand self-serves and ag-supply billboards. Which still beat by miles where he was living after having to sell the house.

Spokane...

Downtown Spokane...

His thoughts turned to the snow swirling in his low-beams, wondering if he'd be able to outrun it. Snowing all the way to Redding from the jawbone he'd heard on the two-way gone quiet a bit ago, nothing he much missed, guys mostly talking about their black-book entries.

All he needed.

A swirl closed in, broke apart in the beams, then a longer one that eased in a lee before heavying up again. Not the most promising of conditions, maybe, but all right with a break or two.

Then the feeling.

Ice, no question: black ice, feathery lightness in the steering, a sense of drifting into the curve instead of adhering to it. Scary as a mother, with 65,000 lbs. of trailer set to follow its own law of physics.

But the tires caught and he breathed again, eased up on the 560 horses, let the big-rig slip back under forty despite the deadline he was fighting. No sleep in the last twenty-two hours, none likely in the next fourteen.

L.A. needing its freaking Christmas trees.

Not that it wasn't good money, it was. All the more, it would help make a dent in his spiraling black-hole nightmare, denizens of which included doctors, anesthesiologists, radiologists—some who'd even managed to sound involved while Ginny lay in there waiting for what never came, a chance.

Which wasn't being fair, but what was...life?

Right.

Frank reached up to his visor and touched the photograph, his favorite of her: sun backlighting her hair, the one where she'd suddenly felt the surf backwashing her feet and laughed at the sensation. The one he'd taken during their trip to the Yucatan.

BL...before the lump.

Frank blinked, threw his attention back to the road. No mystery about where the ice had come from; snowmelt from earlier cascading down the embankment had set up hard and invisible with the plummeting temperature. This before the snow had begun in earnest to clear I-5 of its remaining traffic, nobody else but him fool enough to strap it on in this weather.

The road ghost, he thought, good CB handle.

Frank popped another ephedrine tab, chased it with cold coffee, heard the opening strains of *O Come All Ye Faithful* and punched it off. Had to be careful now to keep it on all-talk, carols becoming harder and harder to steer clear of. He nursed the rig back up to speed. Couple more days...

This time it broke loose for real.

Instantly he backed off, fought the urge to hit the Jake-brake, slow the rig by what amounted to compression—like the brake pedal, a sure way to lock up on ice. Instead he turned toward the skid and hung on, about all he could do, that and hope for a soft hillside. Pray, maybe.

Real future there, alright.

Permanent squelch.

Besides, the future was now. It was like watching another rig in the rearview attempting to pass, only it was his own load, long as a five-story building was tall, jackknifing at the hitch. He was conscious of median and berm beyond the Peterbuilt's nose, slopeoff leading to the river—where the thing that once was a 74-foot tractor-trailer under his control was heading in slow motion, or what seemed like it.

He heard the rig groaning, roadside reflectors snapping off, ice crunching and buckling, buckshot gravel under tires headed sideways. Then the trailer was off the shoulder, tail leading the dog. Rolling and grinding and jolting its way down the slope, an eternity of seconds until the rig tore into firs and pines and cottonwoods, plowing up forest and coming to rest upside down. Close enough for Frank to hear the roar of rapids through the smashed windshield.

Just before he went out.

Freezing cold, the sound of wind adding to the rush of water.

Frank opened his eyes, slowly took inventory: beyond a lump behind his ear, tacky blood in his hair and on his face, nothing felt broken. Then he moved his knee and nearly passed out.

Shit...

Shit, shit, shit.

He appraised it gingerly: nothing crunched and no bones protruding—sprained, likely, or badly bruised. In the faint orange light of the dash, he was able to find his flashlight and scan for damage. The cab looked as if it were a couple of feet shorter, no glass left in any of the windows, this topsy-turvy world. Snow gleamed back at him where it had drifted inside. Luckily, there was no smell of fuel; the tanks hadn't ruptured.

Frank reached for and keyed off the ignition, set the flash down, unharnessed himself, eased into a position where he could reach the CB. Smashed, of course—from the red paint on it, by the fire extinguisher now lying against the dome light.

Anything else in your bag of tricks?
Hell, why stop there?

He checked his watch: 9:07—he'd been out more than thirty minutes. He beamed on the outside thermometer, saw intact dial showing fourteen degrees. Behind him in the mirror, the sleeper cab resembled a Coors can crushed during one of his benders, a fat-trunked pine emerging on either side of the crease. No salvaging anything in there.

Frank reached out what remained of his side window, felt jagged splinters and rough bark. He tried the passenger side and this time punched through, cleared an opening in the snow and eased his banged-up knee out, then head and shoulders. Putting the weight on his right leg, he got to his feet, smelled Christmas trees super strong, and made out his load, dead lumps scattered to the limits of his vision.

Bye-bye payday; hello repo man.

Better if he hadn't come to.

Snowflakes swirled around him, mocked him; the river sounded as if he were standing right in it. Sure enough, his beam picked out brown water moving fast and high, angry through a break in some branches, impressive some other time. As to now, he was beginning to lose feeling in his fingers he was so cold.

He looked back at the Coors can, thought about his parka inside and dismissed it. Might as well be on the moon for all the good it was to him now, cutoff sweatshirt over a tee his sole protection. *Freezing.* He set the flash on a rock, waved his arms to get some feeling back, started sizing up where he stood—beyond his sole asset lying wheels up.

Belly up was more like it.

He shone the light up toward the highway and got only snow; straining to hear, he heard only wind. This late, storm warnings coming all day, they'd have closed the road to traffic, maybe open tomorrow if it let up. Nothing to indicate that from the reports and what he was seeing.

Stay in the cab he'd be ice by morning, assuming anybody could find him under a dump of this magnitude, any sign of his going off where he did long since erased. Slip and slide back up the slope? More like climbing Everest on one leg, and for what—freeze up there, freeze down here. *God, it was cold.* Still, he was considering dragging himself up, taking his chances on a stray smokey or plow, when he cast a glance over his shoulder and saw the light.

Gone in the time it took to blink.

Which figured, of course—the bump on the head. To be certain, Frank turned off his flash and still saw nothing. Then the wind blew a branch out of his line of sight, and there it was again. Enough at least to cancel further debate.

Favoring his knee, Frank started along the river's edge. Footing was treacherous, the snow about two feet deep but powdery, some good in that. The light seemed across the river and up a rise, back from the bank—hard to tell with the snow in his face, eyes watering from the wind. He'd gone about a half mile by his calculation and was about to buy into the irony of freezing ten yards across a river from apparent safety, when he saw the bridge.

Not exactly a bridge, as he drew closer, more suspension apparatus for a pipe running across. But the thing had hand cables, and going slowly he was able to hobble over the torrent, the wind more than once making him think he was going in and how quickly it went to hell on you.

Like with Ginny.

Nineteen years together and *wham*—nothing he could do for her, a dark universe light years distant. Surely not from where he'd *been*, out on the road most of that time, trying to keep them afloat as she drifted away beyond his reach.

Only his life.

Across the river now, he swept the flash around, caught the outline of a trail through weighted trees plopping white. At least the incline was gentle. Gritting for it, taking it slow, Frank kept on until he reached the light, breath burning in his chest and his knee resembling a peg leg, each jolt to it reminding him it wasn't.

The light he'd seen was fixed to the side of an A-frame shed: locked tight, no windows to break, no prospects for shelter. Except maybe on the road winding past it, assuming that was what lay under the drifting white blanket. The one that led to glowing windows about a hundred yards up.

Hands so numb he could barely grip the flash, breath ragged with cold and exertion, Frank lurched the rest of the way—up onto a short porch where he collapsed against the half-log exterior.

The splash of light as the door was opened and someone stepped out was as beautiful as he'd ever seen.

She was bent over him, rubbing his hands and arms, when he jerked awake, saw light brown hair swept upward and back, a face about his age, forty-three. Warm hazel eyes, solid features, cheeks without makeup and flushed with color. Probably from the effort of having to drag him inside, he figured, to where he was propped against a leatherette booth.

"Welcome back," she said.

Long denim skirt, blue-checked blouse inside a navy wool sweater vest. Tallish as she stood back from him, the air smelling of soup and baked things.

"Where are we?" he asked. Easing back the heavy blanket she'd put around his shoulders, the chill in him more or less gone.

"No place much," she said. "Leastwise not anymore, it isn't. Bethany, if you need a name. Nearest town's a good fifteen miles."

She had a voice that fit her, warm with a little crack in it. He glanced over her shoulder.

"This a restaurant?"

"Just my old café, but thanks for the compliment. Least you're not out there."

He leaned against the booth, everything rushing in on him.

"You all right?" Concern in her eyes matching her tone.

"Oh yeah. One good deal after another."

She braced and lent him an arm, and he managed to get up, the knee stiff and aching, a feeling like burn on his hands. He stood, felt dizzy, eased down inside the booth.

"Stay right there," she ordered.

He watched her step behind stools and a counter, fill a ceramic mug, lace it from a brandy bottle underneath. His eyes left her to take in the room: comfortably tidy, half-dozen booths like the one he was sitting in. Chintz curtains and brown oilcloth, rectangular opening through to the kitchen, a thing to put up orders for the cook. Near the register a view container, its glass shelves stacked with pies in various stages of consumption.

She wedged a slab onto a plate, brought it to him with the coffee and brandy, slid in across from him. "Figured you might know what to do with this," she said. "And my name's Claire." Extending a hand he took, noting its warmth and grip.

"Frank." He tried the pie, realized how hungry he was, how good it tasted, some kind of berry. "Thanks," he said after finishing, "What do I owe you?" Sounding inadequate, but wanting to offer.

"Forget it. Looks like you took quite a shot there."

He followed her eyes, touched the spot behind his ear, saw the melting snow was reconstituting the blood. He took the cloth she'd been using and dabbed at it. "Nothing much. Just a bump."

"Mind if I ask why you're here? I mean, at least I've got an excuse."

Grinding metal, snow vortexing in the headlights, the feeling of being worked over with a crowbar.

"My truck hit some ice and went off the highway."

"Lord. You were out driving in this?"

He focused back, swallowed the last of the coffee. "Not much choice in the matter."

She refilled it, this time without the brandy. "Unless you're in jail, it seems to me you always have a choice. Or am I missing something?"

"Not unless you're partial to pulling the wings off flies."

She looked puzzled, the way Ginny had after they'd adjusted her painkillers. Something twinged inside him and let go. "It's a long story, nothing I'm gonna bore you with. Would you have a phone?"

She shook her head. "The lines are down. Only reason we have power now is the generator my husband put in for such as this."

Frank scanned the kitchen, saw no movement, no white apron emerging from a walk-in or shaking snow off. "And would your husband be around?"

"Oh no, he died years ago. It's just us."

"Us..." Frank said.

"Right." Extending a thumb. "You, me, and *her.*"

The girl Claire had gestured to lay on a bunk in a living area off the kitchen. Tiny little thing, her face set in a grimace. Frank could see her swollen abdomen under the blanket lying across her. Limp brown hair, fine-featured face beaded with perspiration.

Her blue eyes left a spot on the ceiling, met his as Claire bathed her face with a damp towel, soothed her with something he couldn't hear. He saw a smile break before she moaned softly and closed her eyes.

He eased back from the alcove, waited for Claire to emerge. On reflex, he tried the phone, heard nothing and put the receiver back.

"She's a runaway off one of the ranches," Claire said, rinsing out the towel. "Came in about the time the phone quit."

"Runaway from what?" Frank asked because it seemed called for.

"From the uncle who did it. Nothing like a ten-mile walk to induce labor."

Great. "How old is she?"

"Fourteen, if she's telling the truth." She squeezed out the towel, dropped it into a pot over a gas flame. "You remember being that age? I hadn't even been kissed yet."

Frank looked at her more closely, saw younger than he'd first imagined, mid-to-late thirties, not bad looking in a country sort of way. "Fourteen's when I started driving trucks, helping out my dad, for all the good it's done." He gestured toward the alcove. "You going to try and get her to a hospital or something?"

"In those drifts? I don't think so." She looked at him. "What..."

He realized he'd been staring. "Just curious. You told her something that seemed to make her feel better. About me?"

"You could say that."

Something in her expression. "Mind if I ask what?"

Pause, the hint of a smile. "The girl's scared to death her baby won't live unless a doctor's present. First words out of her after I got her defrosted." His look must have said it, because she didn't wait for a response, adding, "All you have to do is follow instructions."

"Instructions? What instructions?" The chill suddenly back. "Lady, this is not my problem."

"I'm afraid it is, actually. I told her it was a miracle, a doctor coming here out of that storm."

"You told her—?"

"Please, not so loud. She'll hear you."

"I don't believe this."

"It might be better if you tried."

Holy Flaming Moses. "Lady—Claire—if I'm a doctor, you're the Virgin Mary."

They'd finished the food Claire made. At her insistence, Frank had gone in to try to reassure the girl, act like he knew what he was doing, still ticked at being maneuvered. To his surprise, he hadn't had to say much, just hold her hand until some contractions passed. Back in the dining room, he asked Claire if she had any cigarettes, suddenly feeling the need.

"I wouldn't," she said. "Sorry."

"I'll bet."

"Do you mind? I've midwifed babies. It's going to be fine. Someone may even come by then."

Frank glanced at the windows, the whirl of falling snow, and felt a sensation like the floor dropping out. He forced himself to take a breath, stop pacing, slump in a dining chair.

A moment passed. She said, "Things aren't very good right now, are they? I mean besides your accident."

"Excuse me?"

"Forgive me for being nosy, but I'm getting a feeling it's your wife. You're separated, or she's sick or something."

"I have no idea what you're talking about." As if his voice had atrophied.

"Nothing to be afraid of. Ever since I was a girl, I've had this gift of sight, seeing into people. I've also lost a spouse, remember? It's written all over you."

He let out a breath, ached for a smoke. Too hot in here, too cold to go back outside. *Shit.*

"How long has it been?"

"Lady, with all due respect, that's none of your business."

"Claire. And believe me, it helps."

"*Bullshit, it helps.* Nothing helps."

He watched her drop her eyes to her hands: weathered skin and red knuckles, work and more work. *Perfect.* "Six months and a couple of days. Tomorrow would have been her birthday, so you'll pardon me if—"

"I'm sorry," she said. "Truly."

"Me, too. Helluva day, is all."

She hooked a cloth out of the pot, dipped it in one with cooled water, swirled it around. "What are you going to do about your truck?"

Not liking this direction much better, he said, "Put it this way, I won't be paying off any medical bills for a while. Let alone making truck payments."

She waited, as if knowing more was coming.

Okay, Lady—you want it, you can have it. "Do you have any idea how it feels losing everything? Wishing you'd died too?"

"I think so."

"Yeah, well—sorry to rain on your parade, but I'm not big on miracles right now."

"You're already a miracle to that girl. Did you see how she looked at you?"

"Look—*Claire*—I'm grateful for your help. I've also been called a lot of things, but none so far off the mark."

She sipped coffee.

Hazel eyes regarded him over the lip of her mug.

* * *

"So—what's your sign?" he said after Claire had introduced the girl as Rachel, him to her as *Dr.* Shane, Claire giving him a look like, *That's the best you can do?* Frank trying without luck to recall doctor movies and TV shows he'd seen, stethoscopes about it. The aspirin Claire had given him calming the knee some at least.

"I'm not sure," Rachel said in her girl voice, tightening as a spasm hit and passed. "My birthday is February 23rd."

"Pisces," he said. "Same sign as mine."

Her eyes widened. "That's a good omen, don't you think?"

"I suppose. Have you picked a name for it?"

"Not yet. But I just know it's a boy. Claire agreed with me."

Claire agreed.

"That's nice."

"No, it's—"

With that the power went out.

Dead silence, then Rachel moaning, reaching out for him, Frank taking her hand, feeling the fear in her grip. Claire saying, "Nothing to worry about, just the generator acting up. I've fixed it before."

With his free hand, Frank found his lighter and flicked it on, saw Claire getting a candle from a drawer she'd felt her way to. He leaned the lighter into the wick, watched it flame. Moments later they had a dozen going.

"See," she said, "we don't even need it. You okay, Hon?"

Rachel managed a nod.

"Just like the Boy Scouts," Frank said. "Be prepared?"

"Doctor," Claire said. "Can I have a word with you?"

"I suppose. If Rachel doesn't mind." Trying at least to measure his sarcasm.

They moved out into the dining room.

"I don't like it," Claire said quietly. "It doesn't feel right."

"Well, if you're looking for a second opinion, don't." Shaking out another ephedrine and chasing it with water.

"It's not dilating properly."

"What's not?"

"I can make out the head, but it's not moving down."

"Can't blame it much. Probably terrified."

She ignored the crack.

"All right," he filled in. "What?"

"If things don't improve, we'll have to go in. You've heard of caesarean section?"

Icewater, a look to see she was serious, no sign of not. "Just where does *we* come into this?"

"What I meant was, we could lose them both."

Frank rubbed eyes that felt splashed with road salt, thought about Rachel in there, about Ginny, all of it. *Son of a bitch.*

"He's at it again, isn't he?" Almost to himself.

She glanced up. "Who are you talking about?"

"Who do you think I'm talking about? That is, assuming you're a believer."

There was a pause. "I see. Which I take it you aren't?"

"Let's just say He doesn't fool me anymore."

"And why would you say that?"

"You mean apart from the swell examples in my life?"

She was silent. Taking it for retreat and just on general principle, he added, "Don't get out much, huh? Look around—that girl in there for starters."

"What about her?"

"You sure you want to go there?"

"I don't understand the—"

"Oh, I think you do. See, I know Him by His work. Firsthand. And all the words and all the prayers in the world don't make up for one Ginny Shane. That clear enough?"

"You're angry."

"Lady, you have no idea."

She wrung out the cloths, set them in a row. "I might. I was that way when I lost Sewell. I'm sorry, my husband."

"Okay, I'll bite." His wave having crashed and receded somewhat. "What happened to Sewell?"

"My husband drowned."

"And that's all you're going to say?"

"Years ago, during a flood we had. The bridge was out and I was trying to get across to him. He died trying to save me."

Frank nodded. "Sounds like the big Guy, all right. Real sense of humor."

"I came to terms with it."

"Congratulations."

She paused, unsure how far to take it. Then, "Tell me. What would your wife say about using her like this?"

His turn to hesitate. "I'm alive, she isn't. His call."

"Did you ever consider it might be part of something bigger than you?"

"Ah, the old standby: I don't get it. At least *that* you got right." Sick of it, the pain it brought, but at the same time grounded by the simple act of confronting another human being, the heat of friction after so much empty cold.

God, was he really that needy?

She walked to the window, rubbed a spot in the condensation, looked out at the snow. "That said, are you just going to *let* Him get away with it?"

"What's that mean?"

"Rachel's eaten nothing to speak of in two days. She's already hemorrhaged. She's weak, which means the baby's weak. Even with both of us, they could die. Now, are you going to *let* Him get away with that?"

Frank chewed on it. "Foul up His plan is what you're saying."

"Something like that."

Deep breath. "Lady, I know one thing: I'm too beat to keep this up for long." Not letting on that her idea wasn't lost on him, just that he hadn't thought of it in those terms.

"Does that mean yes or no?"

"*Jesus,*" he said. "Why here?"

Two A.M., the cafe's air dense from steam off the boiling water, Claire still working on Rachel, nothing he could see, thankfully. Rachel's moans had turned to screams, like something out of a horror film. Even Ginny's hadn't been this bad.

"*GOD,*" Rachel screamed. "*GOD OH GOD OH GOD OH GOD OH GOD…*"

Nice work, Frank thought, *hope you're proud of yourself.* He wiped her face with an already damp towel. "Come on Rachel, you're doing fine. Just a little longer."

Frank Shane, M.D. and headcase.

"Doctor," Claire said, tense, but placid by comparison. "I need you down here."

"Say again?"

"I believe you heard me."

"Are you out of your mind?" Lowering his voice.

No response.

"I said—"

"Now, Doctor."

"GOD," Rachel screamed.

"RIGHT NOW."

Taking short breaths, Frank went.

Between two and four, they worked to exploit even the slightest movement, to keep Rachel's efforts in sync—increasingly hard with the contractions she was experiencing—Frank running cloths back and forth from the stove, careful not to skid on the trail of drips. Until Claire said, "See how I have my hands positioned?"

"So?" Well past squeamish by now.

"The cord is prolapsed—pinched in there. Unless we make room for it, the baby gets no blood or oxygen. That's what I've been doing the last two hours. But my hands are cramping. I need you to spell me."

Chill again, despite how far he'd come.

"Did you hear me, Doctor?"

"Yes," Hearing her, but not.

"Frank, I'm losing it."

He looked at his hands, saw nothing remotely capable of this.

"I'll tend to Rachel," she said. "You just do what I was doing. Do you understand?"

He nodded, or something like it, began rubbing one of the cloths over his hands and forearms. *The plan, beat the plan.*

Rachel let out another scream, her voice ragged and getting worse. Claire relinquished her spot and Frank put his hands where hers had been, felt what she described, was aware of the effort she'd been expending to keep the cord free, his own hands all thumbs. And something else: the baby's head moving, nothing he'd felt before, he and Ginny childless. Followed by the rush of what was at stake.

Damn You, I'm a truck driver.

The spasm passed. He was conscious of Claire kneading her hands, shaking them, wiping her face on her sleeve. Saying she'd be right back and hurrying toward the kitchen.

There was a short sharp yell, the sound of falling. Heavily. Long seconds of nothing, then gasps. *Damnit*, the spilled water: he hadn't warned her.

"Are you all right?" he called.

More gasps. Rachel moaning softly.

"Claire?... Talk to me."

She came into view angled against the jamb, her face gray and hard set. Holding her wrist at an awkward angle, the knuckles on her clutching hand white with effort, her voice a whisper through bared teeth: *"Looks like you're it—Doctor."*

From four until dawn it was touch and go, everything going wrong that could, at several points Frank having to let go and rub feeling back into his own hands. Meanwhile, Claire did what she could with Rachel: comforting, coaching, using her good hand to wipe the girl's forehead and give her water. Gritting her own teeth. Directing Frank under her breath. Rachel exhausted beyond noticing, barely able to push when told.

In addition to the cord prolapse, the baby's shoulders wouldn't pass, Frank having to maneuver the slippery wedged form until he could grasp an arm, gently work it around and through. Not wanting to think about the last resort—almost certain they'd lose Rachel. Even money on the baby.

But then at dawn, light beginning to show at the windows, Rachel gave a final push and the baby simply fell into Frank's hands.

A boy.
With no face.
Frank's mouth opened in horror.
"Pay attention. That's the caul," Claire said, "the membrane. You have to remove it. NOW."
God almighty. "How do I—?"
"You make a hole and lift it off. *Gently...that's right.*"
The baby's face appeared; it gasped, took a breath, stopped, began turning blue.
"It's not breathing."
"Check it's mouth."
"Clear," he answered in a voice not sounding like his.
"Listen to me: You're going to have to give it air...puffs, Frank—yes. Wait. Okay, now some more..."
Come on, breathe.
"Again," she said.
Nothing.
"Another set."
Live, Frank thought, don't you dare crap out on me after all this. *"LIVE,"* he heard himself shouting. *"PLEASE."*
And at that, the baby began to breathe.

They sat on the floor with coffee he'd fixed after getting the generator going, nothing really wrong with it, the thing just old. As they sat, they listened to Rachel's deep breathing, watched the small form settle against her. *"Thank you, Doctor,"* she'd said to him as the baby nursed. *"Thank you."* Words that echoed as she and the baby lapsed into exhausted sleep.
Claire raised the wrist he'd wrapped for her. "Feels better, I think. Sure you're not a doctor?"
"Never so sure."
"Lord, I'm tired."
"Yeah," he agreed, although he was still wired from it, the feeling of the baby in his hands, suddenly aware of the day.
Happy Birthday, Ginny.
"Well, you did it," Claire said wearily.
"What's that?"

"Showed *Him*."

Frank let it pass.

"Or did you?"

He smiled at having no ready answer, at the persistence he'd disliked in her about a thousand years ago. He noticed how the glow had returned to her face.

"At least admit it's food for thought," she said.

"Food for thought," he allowed.

He cut pie for them and they ate without speaking, Frank casting frequent glances at the baby. Not quite the first Christmas, but...

Claire finished hers, set her fork down. "They say the caul brings luck. He'll never die by drowning."

"That's a relief."

She rubbed tired eyes. "Sometimes they have the phone lines fixed by daybreak."

He tried, and they did. He dialed his dispatcher first, then the highway patrol, saying he'd meet them at the wreckage and where they'd find it. As he was talking, pacing, he realized how much better his knee was, the limp close to gone. He walked over to Rachel and the baby; after a bit he was conscious of Claire beside him.

"Go ahead, hold him," she said.

"Rachel won't mind?"

"You're her doctor, remember?"

He picked up the baby in its blanket, felt it against him, this tight little ball of muscle. He smelled Rachel's milk, the light sweet fragrance of it. He felt things melting and sliding off.

Claire walked to the window. "Sun's out."

He joined her, all that white difficult to look directly into. "I should be going," he said. "While there's a break."

She went into the living quarters, came back with a plaid wool coat. "You're about Sewell's size. You're welcome to it." Handing it to him, taking the baby in return.

"Are you sure?"

"No one's worn it but him," she said. "I'm sure."

He put it on, felt its rough heft, looked at her nodding, the baby at her shoulder, a kind of radiance about them. "Since Ginny, I'm not very big on goodbyes."

"Since Sewell, neither am I." Taking the hand he offered. "You did fine in there, Frank. You know that, don't you?" Eyes scanning his face, as though trying to memorize it.

"Other way around."

"No. She made it because of you, let that in. Now go."

She opened the door and let him out, closed it quickly so as not to chill the baby. Frank stood on the porch. And suddenly the something that had been bothering him popped into his mind. He turned back, but the sun was bright on the windows, making it hard to see in.

"I never told you my last name." Raising his voice and squinting through the glass. "When you introduced me as Dr. Shane. How'd you know it was Shane?"

"I just knew," he heard her say.

"I don't—"

He couldn't see them at all then. Just the brightness.

"Happy Christmas, Frank. Have a good life."

He opened his eyes to piercing sun, a tapping at the window.

"You okay in there?"

With effort, Frank uncoiled from the position he'd stiffened into; he saw blue sky, endless snow, a salt-and-pepper CHP. Dark sunglasses, breath showing around his face.

"I said, are you okay?"

Frank rolled down his window to air like ice.

"I think so." Checking his watch: more than ten hours he'd been out. A snowplow clanked by on the highway. About the way he felt.

"Looks like you played a little crack-the-whip. Lucky you didn't end up in the river."

Frank touched his head where it hurt, a crust of dried blood.

"Lucky to be wearing that coat, too. Case you didn't notice, it got down to four degrees last night."

Frank felt the wool plaid, thick under his fingers.

"Can you start it up?"

"What's that?"

"See if she'll run. You sure you're okay?"

Ignition. He reached for the keys, turned them, felt the engine catch, settle into idle.

The patrolman nodded.

"Thanks," Frank said.

"You need anything?"

"Not that comes to mind." Still trying to shake it off, figure out what the—

"Anytime you're ready, then."

The CHP wrote something in his notebook, stowed it, started crunching toward his car.

"Officer?" Frank called after him. "Excuse me. Are you familiar with the area?"

"I should be," he said, turning back. "Grew up in Dunsmuir down the road."

"The name Bethany ring a bell? Tiny place with a café?"

He puzzled on it. "No, I don't—wait a minute...right. Across the river?"

"That's the one," Frank said, glad for at least some frame of reference. Not everything, but a start.

"I doubt it," the CHP said. "Bethany got wiped off the map when their reservoir broke. Years ago. Saw pictures of it once. Nothing left but the foundations."

Frank just stared. "But it's there. I was there."

"Some other life, maybe. Water drowned everybody, except for a baby they found. A boy."

The caul. The caul brings luck.

"I remember my granddad talking about it. Kid grew up to be a doctor. Delivered lots of the locals back then."

He'll never die by drowning.

"Son, you sure you're all right?"

Frank nodded, though it took a second.

"I was you, I'd have that bump looked at when you hit a clear exit. Plows are doing what they can, but don't expect miracles."

"Say that again?"

"Just take it slow."

Frank watched him get into his unit, swing around after the snowplow, over a rise and gone. For a while he sat there, all of it washing over him. Then there was nothing left but to head out. He reached up and touched Ginny's picture, told her he loved her, not to worry about him anymore. That he'd be okay.

He'd put it in gear, was about to let out the clutch, when his gaze drifted again across the drop-off, to the river and the trees beyond. Even with the sun in his eyes, that had to be, *had to be*, a wisp of smoke curling up from where Bethany lay.

Foreword to
The Seam

J.L. Abramo

Having successfully penned three full-length novels, I imagined that writing a short story would be a walk in the park. Therefore, I gladly accepted an invitation to contribute to a private-eye short-story anthology entitled *Fedora III*. I discovered that completing the assignment was no simple task. Regardless of the fact that Richard Barre makes creating a fully realized, engrossing, and beautifully crafted work of short fiction look like a piece of cake.

With *The Seam,* Barre offers us another of his wonderful Christmas-themed stories with a supernatural twist. The seam is a coal vein beneath the Kentucky ground. The seam is the strong stitching that holds a family together. *The Seam* is a gift to the reader, a period piece as timeless as the spirit of Christmas itself.

As writers, we are encouraged to *"write what we know."* Richard Barre was born in Los Angeles and raised in California, but his descriptions of the underground mines and the lives of the Kentucky coalminers who lived and died in those mines in the early 1900s would have the reader believe that Barre had lived in that time and place himself. Perhaps he had.

My uncle told me a story when I was young. He was asleep in bed when he heard his mother, long deceased, call out to him. He woke to find her standing before him, urging him to get out. He jumped from his bed to discover that there was a fire in the apartment, and he escaped to safety. I did not doubt then, nor do I now, that his mother came to warn him. Richard Barre has that ability to make the supernatural seem very natural.

More than just an adventure and a coming-of-age tale, *The Seam* is also a testament to the importance of family and to the importance of being able to count on those we need to depend on. Ethan's grandfather is an uneducated man, but a very wise man, who tells his grandson, "A miner don't never leave his fellows in the mine, he'd die first. See how often you run across that above ground."

The Seam

Frankfort, Kentucky
December, 1958

The white sheets remind me of kites.

Lost in my research, I've been unaware the storm has moved so close. If my neighbor doesn't take them in off her line soon, they'll not only be wet, but ice. Now they merely flap against the blackening sky.

Black. There's a color I understand.

I reach for the cigarettes my doctor has forbidden me. But another glance at those sheets, that sky, makes me pause, and I move instead toward the bookcase, castors on my desk chair squeaking where I've been meaning to oil them. Bottom shelf, right side, scuffed dry leather. Dust that rises as I swipe it off and open the album since God knows when.

Like everything else in my life, the photographs have faded with age. The memories, however, are another story.

I lift the cover and see it again, the mountain behind our house my grandaddy always said could have been put there by our family. That's how much coal he and his brothers, my daddy and his brother, took out from under it. Me, I suppose, before I broke with it and got into mining law then to legislating it.

To make a long story short.

Eastern Kentucky
The Cumberland
December, 1907

Rain fell cold and steady the day my daddy and uncle came home for good. It sluiced from the eaves, spattered on the canvas bags, one tagged *Curtis Earl Garland*, the other *Errol Todd Garland*, the company men carried up the steps and into the house. It drummed on the pine coffins they brought by later so Daddy and Uncle Errol could lay proper on saw horses in the living room, candles burning at each end.

"Sorry for your loss, but it's a blessing," the men said on their way out. "Mr. Woolfort will be in touch."

Mean as it was, the rain created a kind of curtain around us so that my mother's mournful cries, my grandaddy's already-racked face, the wet or wide eyes of my four sisters, were our own and nobody else's.

In coal country you learned a blessing was where you found it.

That night the rain turned to sleet and ice, the house creaking under its weight. From where I lay in bed, staring at the candles making moving shapes on our ceiling, it sounded like Daddy and Uncle Errol shifting in their coffins, wondering, like us, what had happened to bring them to such.

Later we learned from Mr. Woolfort that a black powder shot packed by a crew that had run out of clay and used mud instead had blown back and touched off the dust on everything, making Daddy and Uncle Errol part of what they were bringing down.

That night, however, there were only the creaks.

I should have known it was the mine calling me.

It called, you went: that's the way it was then.

Those able to pick up the slack did, even if that was me and eleven years old. But eleven then wasn't eleven now, soft living and know-how about nothing. I'd already been three months sorting at the tipple, where the coal was processed for loading, separating out the slate and limestone as the coal shook its way down the sizing screens, past some younger than I was. The whole structure rattling and screeching so bad you took the noise home with your dinner pail. Point is, I was already bringing in money to help out.

But now, it was me or nothing.

A foreman who'd been friends with Daddy and Uncle Errol and knew Grandaddy was seized up with the *rheumatiz* as he called it, lung trouble on top, Mama with four younger girls to see to, recommended to Mr. Woolfort I start tending mules. Them or the floor-to-ceiling doors that shunted the flow of air through the mine's forty miles of tunnels.

The fans generating the air were big, almost as big as our house. You could hear them a mile away down in Seraphim where we lived, just up from Christmas Creek, which darkened its bed with coal effluent, grayed the washes of Seraphim, and gave the mine its name.

Christmas Creek, shafts four and seven.

Owners: Amalgamated & Eastern Kentucky Mining Company.

Headquartered up in Louisville.

Anyway, some trapper boy—the kids who tended the doors were called that—fell asleep and men stopped drawing air. Down there you did your job or people died. Often enough even when you did.

We buried my father and uncle in the cemetery up the rise behind our wood-frame house—nothing fancy, just one in a row with daylight basements and steps up. Ice on the road and our breath smoking in the cold air, Father Buell already running late for the next burial, three men who'd died with them when the shot blew out.

I was trudging down the hill afterward, feeling lost, when Grandaddy fell in step beside me. As bad as he felt, he said, he didn't blame the mine, nor should I. A mine was no better or worse than how it was worked. Just happened to be underground.

"Surface people don't understand it and never will." Going on to explain that despite a weak one now and again, miners were links in a chain, men you could rely on when the you-know-what hit the fan. That on top of it, his rheumatiz or whatever was bothering him that day never afflicted him as bad down there as up top.

He didn't say these things around my mother, who, in light of what happened, had a less-than-favorable view. Understandably, she was a good deal more willing to attribute the mess we now found ourselves in to statements like those spouted by her father-in-law.

"Tell you one thing, Ethan," he'd say when we were off in the woods squirreling or something, perhaps a bit defensively. "A miner don't never leave his fellows in the mine, he'd die first. See how often you run across that above ground."

He was something, my grandad. Elvin Grover Branch Garland: Grover not after President Grover Cleveland, but this collie dog his daddy and mama loved enough to name him after. He loved Grover himself the years they'd had together, never considered the name a drawback, though he had to defend it a time or two in school. Some kids were just jealous, he figured. He even encouraged my mama and daddy to name me after a dog they liked, but they'd never had one like Grover and thus declined.

So Ethan Delane Garland I became, Delane being Mama's family name down in Smith's Ridge, where Daddy courted her. Fifteen she was when he uprooted her for the coal. Schuylkill County hard then Ohio and West Virginia soft before following the bituminous and Grandaddy into the Cumberland. I was five when he'd moved us all to Seraphim, *that* name surely someone's idea of a joke. That or it had looked a whole lot different before the old-growth timber had gone to shore up the tunnels.

Grandaddy was the one I talked to. Sisters, school, things in general. For one thing, Daddy and Uncle Errol were gone six in the morning until eight at night, six days a week, and Mama always was too busy with the girls. For another, Grandaddy knew how to listen as well as talk. Most people never come close to figuring that one out.

His hands were bent by countless breaks; a long-ago accident from when he was a fire boss testing a spur for gas had left him with burns on his face and arms. People not our family whispered about him being disfigured, but never around me, at least not a second time. With us, it was two souls, his that knew things and mine eager to. Occasionally

I'd find him down at Leggett's Store, playing checkers with the retired miners, less so as those his age became fewer.

I guess he hadn't many people to talk to either.

All said and done, his words in my ears and the hat they'd passed around for us not getting any bigger, I went to work for real.

Shafts four and seven had been slopers until the slopes got so long the company decided shafts and hoists were a quicker way of getting the miners to the coal seam. Nine hundred feet down, four stacked cages, each with ten miners standing shoulder to shoulder, their pit-lamps fluttering. Time was money, so the square of daylight was gone in seconds. Seepage splashed from the shaft walls, then the hoist operator set us down, one cage out at a time. My first time.

I tried to make sense of it: miners dispersing in teams, me looking down the tunnels marked only by the occasional headlight or lamp flame. Like night lit only by fireflies, you made it out and you didn't. Sounds didn't travel the way I expected, they were muffled. A constant sixty degrees, the air smelled of wet rock and earth, lamp carbide and sulfur, timber pitch and mold. Plus it was heavy, like the mountain itself was resting on your chest. On mine, anyway.

I started for the foreman's shed.

I was small for my age, so they had me on door duty the first few months, not leaving me to anything might get me run off the paycheck. Opening doors for the loaded cars on their way to the hoist before securing them to maintain the air flow, some places strong enough to blow your cap off and your lamp out.

It made me feel good to see the same sights, smell the smells, hear the crunch of boots on coal dust, the same throb of groundwater pumps Daddy and Uncle Errol had. One of the miners who knew them took me to where it had happened, but by then the face had moved another fifty yards in. And yet, enveloped by a black so alive I swore it breathed, coal flecks gleaming in the light of my pit-lamp, hiss of natural gas sounding like water over stones, I felt close to them. So close I was glad the friend of my daddy's couldn't see my face for the tears on it.

But the mine, I would learn, ran with tears.

Christmas Creek wasn't supposed to be good fishing because of what the mine flushed into it, but every now and then we caught one. It gave us an excuse one Sunday, Grandaddy and me, to talk after church. Daddy and Uncle Errol fifteen months in the ground, Mama taking in sewing and wash and tending the girls, me thirteen and still not growing. It was a clear fall day, trees in the hollow all yellow and red, their leaves on the creek, the air crisp as a bite into a crabapple.

"You think I ever will?" I asked him. "Get bigger, I mean."

It was a question Mama would handle with *That all you got to worry over, you take Comet down to Leggett's right now for beans and flour.* Which, of course, is why I asked Grandaddy.

Comet was our mule, rescued from mine duty by my father, who'd grown attached to him. Other than a limp from a runaway one-and-a-half ton that had severed his harness on its way to maiming two loaders against a brace, Comet was fine. Ready to do it again, I always thought, if that was what it took to escape the darkness.

Grandaddy knocked the ash from his pipe, something he was in no way allowed with his lung condition. After a cough and two more, a hack and a spit, he said, "Your daddy was full size?"

"Yes, sir," I answered. "He was that."

"Mama full size?"

"For a woman, I guess."

"And me—am I full size?"

I regarded him. He was stooped from his years down there and the rheumatiz, but I wasn't about to say it. Besides, unstooped I suppose he was close to Daddy's height.

"What? You think your own grandad would fib about something that important?"

He'd fib in a wink to josh me, but shaking my head no seemed the best idea, so that's what I did.

"Took me till I was fifteen—short's an advantage down there," he said. "No dwarfs is where I'm going with this, Ethan. You with me? Not in this family."

"Yes, sir. No dwarfs."

"Then I expect you'll be sprouting up in no time."

I took a moment with my next question, something that had begun to worry me even more than height.

"You mean, like everything will?" Casual-like: friends Johnny Combes and Verron Recker quick to ask and smirk when I told them no, it hadn't yet grown. Not quick enough myself to fib.

He looked amused, coughed to hide it. "The whole package, son. Just be patient."

My relief, I'm sure, was tangible.

"So it's like fishing," I said at length, having learned about similes from Miss Fencik down at the school and wanting to tell her I'd come up with one. I liked Miss Fencik. That is, before I quit for the mine.

Grandaddy said, "Never heard it compared to that, but why not? Damn sure need patience in this creek."

The stream murmured, sun filtered through the leaves; I smelled wood smoke drifting up, someone firing an early stove. Fall was the best season, far from the outhouse smells and mine haze of summer, the dust caked to your sweat.

"Ethan, you trailing Murtaugh and Shoney, yet?"

I was taken aback; I hadn't told anyone of my promotion, not even Johnny Combes. He saw my look and spoke to it. "Your old grandad still has some pull left in his mule. Give me some credit."

Guessing he'd talked to Mr. Woolfort, I told him I started Monday: apprentice loader, bird dogger, lamp charger— whatever my new team required. Ten cents more an hour, as the spread of black on my face and clothes would soon announce.

He stared at the riffle, our lines where they sat weighted with split shot. Finally, "Ethan, you make me proud, you know that? Just...damn...proud."

It was the finest thing anyone would say to me.
Then or ever.

To Mama's chagrin, Grandaddy had used his savings one year to buy her and Daddy a camera, the impracticality of such a gift, let alone the film it would eat up, sticking in her craw. No nonsense, that was Mama. The family grew up, you remembered—camera, indeed. Yet she seemed to take pleasure in the result, mounted black-and-whites of whatnot and whomever inside the photo book he'd also splurged to buy.

The book whose pages I turn now as rain sweeps the window, the sheets beyond it thrashing about in the storm, tethered doves.

And there I am in 1911.

Almost done with fourteen, still pint-sized in my pit-lamp and hat, working coat and trousers. Posed outside our porch I had yet to fix.

I turn the page, see one with me and Mama, Rosalie and Emma, Maryalice and Letty, at a creek picnic, Grandaddy behind the lens.

Then one of me in a mood best left forgotten...

I'd just had a row with Mama over whether Letty, a baby when Daddy and Uncle Errol died—now four and more than able, I thought—was capable of reaching the outhouse on her own. This after I'd banged a knee almost to the point of leaving my shift to soak it in Epsom. Cold rain turning the new snow to foot-deep slush.

Ordinarily I'd have carried her and no questions, but fatigue and hurt had their way in my refusal. Or maybe it was how Mama asked it. Like the book I was trying to master had no more import to her than I did.

Anyway, I tromped around, blowing off like an airshaft, finally carrying Letty outside, waiting while she did her business, carrying her back to bed, my knee hurting and Mama not speaking to me. I was feeling sorry for myself down in the basement, trying to smoke a cigarette I'd hand-rolled, cold air coming in from where I'd yanked open a window for ventilation—*I'll smoke if I damn please*—when Grandaddy came down.

The trip was an effort for him. By then his health was failing and he stood puffing and sallow-faced in the dim light that accentuated it. He wiped his brow, settled in against the work table where I'd used my growing mine skills to fashion Mama a crude sewing table.

He took a moment to recover his breath, then said, "She doesn't mean it, your mama. It's anger over your daddy and uncle that hasn't leached out yet."

"She means it," I said, the idea of Mama not meaning something nonsense. "She means everything she says. If it came to it, she'd take Comet over me."

"You ever think she's that way because she knows you can take care of yourself while the girls can't? That she's treating you like the man of the family?"

"No, I have not."

It was an honest sentiment; never had such occurred to me. I'd covered my heat with smoke, had gotten a lungful down without choking, when he said, "Ethan, your mama was a girl herself once, had herself a smile like spring. Lot like that little one you been eyeing at church."

Like Annie Monhegan?

A paperwhite against the dead leaves of winter?

I objected.

"Maybe even prettier," he threw in.

That did it. I had the sense he was baiting me, but I could take no more. He let me get as far as the base of the steps.

"Before you go up to apologize, as I know you are, I want to tell you something. It's about people. Families in particular."

I stopped, curious despite my pique. Though we'd been talking less and less as my responsibilities grew—other interests, if I were to admit it—he was still my grandad. Besides, my knee was stiff and it would not be the stormy exit I wished.

He said, "You know when your mother sews how a seam sometimes is stronger than the fabric around it?"

"So?" Determined to hold my ground.

"Families are like quilt patches stitched together. Only a fool rips them apart without care or leaves them to rot. You understand what I'm telling you here?"

I had a short but deliberate drag before putting out my spite smoke.

"Thought you might," he said. "I'll be up in a minute to wrap that knee for you. Go on and git. I know it's paining you."

As I limped upstairs to put it right with Mama, I thought I caught him grinning.

But the lesson he took such pains to impart struck rock before rooting in soil. Though Mama and I came to terms, the mine and its fourteen-hour shifts took all I had, which seemed to everyone else in my family like everything, the snappish moods I brought home.

Looking back on it, I was simply exhausted.

Living it, I found fault with everyone and everything.

Even my grandad.

Thin and sick as he'd become, he insisted on attending church, and it fell to me to escort him. Gone were the days when we'd fish and talk, hunt and talk, laugh and talk. Nobody's fault, just life, I told myself. Or maybe I was learning what Mama had been going through those four years since they'd scraped Daddy and Uncle Errol off the seam.

Anyway, that particular Sabbath I'd slept through Mama rousing the girls to early mass so she could come home and finish a dress she'd promised Mrs. Shalinsky next door. I scrabbled around, left without breakfast; Grandaddy on my arm, we arrived just as mass got under way. As it progressed, I saw Annie Monhegan several rows up. I was admiring her profile, the light in her hair, when I saw her turn and catch me at it.

I looked away, looked back.

To my amazement, she smiled at me.

Instantly, everyone else in boxy, drafty St. Catherine's of the Hollow vanished in the rush of emotions sweeping me before it. Everyone, I realized to my horror, but Grandaddy, who had drifted off and whose gray head had just then come to rest on my shoulder.

I flushed a red she had to have seen from her seat.

It was the basis of her smile, I was certain.

My drooling and now-snorting grandfather.

The snort became a spasm of coughing that jerked him awake, gasping and hacking. As we stumbled from the row, every head in the congregation turned toward us, Annie Monhegan's included, I did the unthinkable.

I fled.

I suppose I wasn't gone long, just down to the creek for some breaths and to hurl a rock or two. But when I got back, I found him sitting on the church steps, the mass over and Father Buell beside him. They were talking in hushed tones I could tell were serious until I scuffed up beside him. He smiled at me, though Father Buell didn't.

I must have looked as guilty and awful as I felt.

"Grandaddy, I—"

But he was quicker: "Like I said, I asked Ethan there to run home and get my tonic. Turns out I don't need it after all." This to Father Buell, whose look softened somewhat.

"Don't worry about a thing, Elvin," Father Buell told him, standing to go inside. "It's in the hands of the Lord."

"It's not His hands I worry about," Grandaddy said back. "You have everything you need for right and proper?"

"I believe we've covered everything."

"No belief about it." The handkerchief still clutched in his fist. "Either you have the means or you haven't."

"I have, most certainly," Father Buell said, with a sideward glance at me. "Now put your mind at rest and let the boy take you home."

"Father, this boy's as much man as you'll see in these parts or anywhere. Now I bid you good day."

When we were out of earshot I finally found the courage to say what had been a stone around my neck, my failing him and the shame I felt, but he waved it off.

"We all got our moments, Ethan. Thank God more than one to get judged by or I'm headed to where I deserve."

"I don't—"

"Sure you do, son, you got eyes. If I could just go off like some old dog and not trouble anybody, I would. But, knowing His ways I'd just lie there till somebody fell over me and broke something of theirs or mine."

"Grandaddy, you're not—"

"Dying? Everybody is, son, don't take it personal." His arm coming around me the first time in a while. "Besides, it's not how you die as how you work your seam. Keep it in mind."

In the days leading up to Christmas and my birthday on the 24th, Grandaddy rallied, even to walking with me the see the few decorations Seraphim boasted. They seemed to raise his spirits to where it was almost like old times. We even set up a chair so he could watch me fish one of the pools where I'd had some luck, though not that day.

Still, I kept casting.

"So how's it going down in seven," he asked from behind his muffler and ear flaps. "Murtaugh and Shoney treating you right?"

"Yes, sir." Not knowing how I felt about what he'd told me, his dying, pushing it as far back as I could. "Got me rolling squibs already."

"Lord, I knew their fathers," he said. "What about Mr. Woolfort?"

"Okay, I suppose."

"He got you working on your birthday?"

"Nothing I didn't choose myself. Figured Mama and the girls might appreciate me around for once on Christmas instead of working."

But he'd drifted past it, much as my line had its entry splash.

"Lord, what I'd give to turn back the clock," he said.

"You liked it down there that much?"

"You don't, Ethan? I was thinking you did."

I said nothing, recast my line.

"I see," he finally said. "Might need to compare it with other jobs, whether or not they're worth it. How being alone really feels."

"Alone...I don't—"

"That's how it is on top, Ethan. You don't know it yet, but you will. Down there, you ain't ever alone. You can always see other lights, know there's men behind 'em." He coughed into his handkerchief, glanced at it, stuck it away. "You get that little girl of yours a present yet?"

Annie Monhegan and I had gone walking after a Sunday dinner she'd asked her folks to invite me to at their place. Food not as good as Mama's, but good enough when you considered who was across the table from me.

"Licorice," I said. "Not much, but something."

"She's as pretty as your mom was, Ethan. I ever tell you that?"

I smiled at him.

The quiet between us was a sound I still hear.

Morning of the 24th, I was beat before even hearing the mine whistle. Grandaddy'd had a bad night, his coughing keeping me awake. But he was in the kitchen when I came in to fill up my dinner pail, Mama already back to bed after setting it out.

"Got everything you need?" he asked me over coffee, his voice little more than a rasp now.

"Yes, sir." Same as every pre-dawn morning, me eager as ever to carry on a conversation.

"Wicks for your lamp?"

"Here."

"Ethan, I ever tell you that coal seam you're working once was just ferns and plants and decay? Peat bog that pressure made something special?" Eyes unnaturally bright in the pale hollow of his face.

I thought, if only I had a nickel for the times.

"Yes, sir, you did at that."

"Getting so I don't remember what I say when I say it." He coughed into his rag, caught his breath, reached into his robe for something. "Happy Birthday, Ethan. Wish it could be more."

The envelope he handed me was string-sealed and stained and held a cluster of yellowed photographs I had no time to get into with him. Fact was I yawned, though not meaning to.

"Man should know who he comes from," he said. "I wrote everybody on the backs, the Garlands anyhow. Some on my mama's side I wasn't sure of."

"Thank you," I said, half of me already out the door. "Look at them later?"

"They ain't going anywhere."

We finished our coffee. He said he wished he was going down with me, just like he said every morning. I patted his hand and took off for the bridge across the creek.

As it turned out, three hundred sixty were going down with me that day and the line for the cages was long, wind off the ridge as mean as you'd felt or wanted to. Going down to sixty degrees, the men were actually chatty despite no such thing as morning light that time of year. Some actually hummed and sang.

At bottom, Murtaugh, Shoney and I teamed up with an extra loader named Hawes and an extra shot-man named Talcott. Extra because month's end was coming and our shift quota was running behind, the idea being to bring down as much coal as we could load in a day plus some for tomorrow's skeleton shift. We trudged through several doors, their trapper boys all looking enviously at me, about a mile to the foreman's shed. We read the fire boss's slate that everything checked out gas-wise in our particular spot, then we walked to it, a crosscut between chambers angled slightly upwards of the haulway.

Murtaugh and Talcott set to drilling the face while Shoney timbered up a ceiling spot the fire boss had marked with chalk. Hawes and I began loading day-before coal and in an hour had it cleared and sent off. By then Talcott was ready with the squibs and charges they'd ignite; after packing them, we retreated down the chamber. All around us we could hear whumps like distant cannon as similar shots were set off.

When ours went, I could tell something was wrong by virtue of how far into the chamber the coal had blown, some thirty feet where eight or ten might be the most expected. In addition, where they'd tamped seven-foot charge-holes, the blasts had only removed four feet of coal. The charges had blown back out more than across the seam as intended.

At least Talcott's section had.

Murtaugh swore and laid into Talcott; Talcott lashed back with profanities to the point that Shoney and Hawes had to pull the men apart. Bad blood going back, Hawes told me later under his breath. Nonetheless, by lunchtime we had the coal that had fallen picked into loadable size. We'd carted it, all but the fine. No time for that since Talcott already had us behind schedule, Murtaugh said, when the replacement cars arrived.

I set the brakes, drove wedges under the wheels, stood by.

Murtaugh then said everyone could take lunch except Talcott, who he expected to redrill and repack the holes and to hell with his lunch, he could take it when a moment presented, not that Murtaugh much cared. Talcott had a grip on his pick handle and looked ready to take Murtaugh's head off, but Murtaugh faced him down and we retreated to a tapped-out chamber to eat and drop leftovers on the mine rats we'd grown partial to.

I fed one I'd named Big-Boy Bob after a mule driver who'd picked on me and later wound up kicked in the head by one. Miners looked to the rats to warn of impending cave-in. When the rats hightailed it, the miners did, too; point being, they didn't mind them. Though when I was tending mules, they presented a problem competing for their oats, what drew them down there in the first place.

Anyway, our break was almost up when Murtaugh said he'd better check the job. Shoney and Hawes's exchanging glances told me "the job" meant Talcott, that they'd better be on hand in case it came to separating them again. I was getting up when Shoney waved me back down, said when I'd finished eating to see about flagging down more cars. That if he knew Talcott, this time should do the trick. Winking to drive the point home that it would be the last slack moment *we* saw that day.

I wasn't keen to miss Talcott's blast, but I went.

I must have put a half mile between us, having diverted two more cars with a possible third promised, eager to return, when I heard it: an explosion like nothing I'd heard before, multiplied by a hundred.

God, oh God.

My team...

I'd flashed that the son of a bitch had touched off the face and the dust and everything in the chamber and beyond when the cannon he'd fired blew me ass over, out with my lamp.

I have no recollection how long I was out, but the world in which I awoke, stuffed in behind a smashed and overturned coal car, was far from the one I'd left. This one was pitch black, fire hot, smothering. I lay gasping against a track in rushing effluent—the big pipe suctioning out groundwater had burst. I could tell from the smell of sulfur filling the haulway that somewhere the seam still burned.

Jesus, Mary and Joseph...

No sound but the water, my own groan as I tried moving my shoulder. And whether I could smell it or not, I knew what followed mine explosions and fires: gas—blackdamp that killed within seconds. I fumbled for my cap and lamp, felt nothing but water and debris. A wave of dizziness sucker-punched me. I felt warmth running on my face, touched it, tasted blood. I lost my lunch, my shoulder screaming with the retching.

I was finished.

I give you my heart and my soul.

And then I saw it.

* * *

The light bobbed toward me, vanished as its wearer scanned for survivors, reappeared as his lamp faced me again, closed the gap between us. I heard myself cry out, saw the lamp pause as though an ear had been cocked against the water sounds.

"*Here,*" I shouted, or what passed for a shout.

The light came forward, paused as it spotted me. I made out a face about my age, at least I thought it was, under the black. The eyes were young and he was about the same size I was.

"You able to walk?" a voice that could have been my own asked.

"Think so." Standing, weaving until he steadied me.

"There any more down that way?"

"Don't know. Don't see how."

"I was asleep, but don't tell nobody. You know who set it off?"

"My team, I think," the admission paining me worse than the shoulder. "Leastwise they were set to."

He nodded. "That cart there took what you would have. We got to get out of here."

"Can't leave them. I—"

"Nothing to leave. Blast jammed everything up for miles, more dead than I could count coming down. They'll be sealing the shafts to kill the fires, so you know we haven't much time. Only way out's one I know, but it's far. Think you can make it?"

One lamp between us and me nearly passing out every time I moved my shoulder.

He sniffed the air. "Blackdamp's coming," he said. "You want to live, grab hold of my belt."

We stumbled along the tracks, me behind him, for what seemed like miles: mules, men and boys sprawled around roof-falls and derailed trips. At one point I had to rest, and he reluctantly stopped.

"Am I going to have to carry you?" he said.

"Who are you?"

"Nobody much. You're Garland, though, I seen you around. And my lamp ain't got long, so don't get comfortable."

Comfortable...slumped against fallen slabs nearly blocking the tunnel, dead rats floating in the foot-deep water, the roof cracking ominously beyond our one flame. I just looked at him.

"See your point," he said. "Got some climbing to do 'fore we're done. That is, if we're lucky."

We passed more rock falls, some with passage barely permitting one at a time, my shoulder screaming in protest. Some tunnels held corpses beyond recognizing, others intact bodies in the act of eating or work, as if a sudden pressure had suspended them in time and space. One miner's watch still ran where it had been hung on a peg.

"My God," I let out. "Hell could be no worse."

"Implosion," my guide said as we turned for yet another slope. "Pressure differential. Deadly as any explosion or gas."

"How you come to know so all-fired much?"

"Started when I was eight and seen about all I hope to, friend. You plan to make it, breathe shallow into your coat and walk."

Fact was, I was already feeling weak and achy, the first signs of blackdamp. I lost all sense of time and direction, one tunnel after the next, flat leading to gradual then steeper inclines, short painful breaths. It felt like a hand had reached into my chest and made a fist.

"That brattice there," he said finally. "You see it?"

I followed his weakening beam. The explosion had left a crack in one of the barriers sealing off a part of the mine no longer worked. Picturing us wandering until we dropped, no closer to rescue than the moon's dark side, I said, "You know the abandoned tunnels?"

"Told you, I started young. You coming or not?"

"Won't they have a fan running soon?" Too weak even to cough.

"Not till they're sure the fires are out. They flare up, they'll lose the whole thing. Not that you'll care."

* * *

It was a struggle—once through, him directing me to stuff my coat in the crack against the gas. Though musty, the air inside was breathable and blessedly cooler. I began following with greater purpose, not that it was much. Seepage dripped from the walls and tunnel roof, coursed in the grooves left when the tracks were removed to serve the working tunnels.

He stopped, cocked his head.

"You feel that?"

All I felt was wet, hurt, lightheaded, spent. Then, Great God Almighty, a rush of cold air from up the tunnel. Heaven sending us its breath. "Sweet Lord," I think I said.

"Toadhole. Thought it might be there."

Toadholes were sinkholes that mothers warned their kids about because they could and did fall through into the headings. I'd nearly lost a friend to them once. We'd been clowning around this not very big one and Rory Miggins had fallen through, broken his pelvis, and had to be extracted by rope. Rory never had walked right after it.

No matter. From this end, any toadhole seemed blessed.

My companion pulled me along to where a cold rivulet splashed from a ceiling crevice onto a buildup of rock fall. He said, "That slit up there's where it's coming in. Already dark outside or we'd see it better."

My heart sank. Unless it widened back of the slit—unlikely since the surround was limestone and the cascade already had dislodged a fair amount of loose rock—we were done. Not only was the toadhole unreachable, we had no tool to work it.

"Lamp's about empty, too," he said to my look. "Going to kill the flame for when we need it."

The darkness was like a coffin lid. When my eyes adjusted, I could just see the slit by passing my hand in front of it, charcoal on black. But by then the standstill had set me to shivering.

"Need to sit down," I said.

"Pass out and never get up you mean. Yell. It'll warm you."

I did, for what seemed a long time.

"No use," I said, finally. "Just want to—"

"You know any carols?"

Christmas was the last thing on my mind. Birthday, any of it.

"Not much of a singer," I said.

"Might be different enough to attract attention. Somebody has to be up there. With me, now: *Adeste Fidelis*."

I did the best I could, the croak my voice had become. Shoulder stabbing me on the high notes, one carol after another. Like all of Kentucky had to hear it, not just Seraphim.

Somewhere between *Good King Wenceslas* and *O Tannenbaum*, he touched my arm, told me to shut up and listen. I did and, from the light of the lamp he'd relit as a signal, returned his grin at the faint shouts coming down through the toadhole.

They said it was just me down there when they broke through.

Babbling that I wouldn't leave without him, the kid with the pit-lamp and the coal-black grin, their lights revealing no one all the way back to the brattice where my coat still held back the gas.

Not that they hung around long.

Giving me a knockout so I'd stop fighting the lift-out they put me on.

I heard someone say the word "miracle," then I was floating in air.

A hundred made it out, me being the hundredth.

THE GREAT CHRISTMAS CREEK MINE DISASTER.
TWO-HUNDRED SIXTY DEAD.
CHIEF MINE INSPECTOR TO REPORT.

Mama and the girls were all over me when I was brought home, my shoulder tight in a sling, burns greased down under bandages.

"We made you honeycake," Letty said as they stood there beaming. "Your favorite."

"Where's Grandaddy," I croaked.

Mama shook her head. "Stopped breathing about the time we felt the ground move and heard the whistles. I'm real sorry, Ethan. Guess I know what he meant to you. We found this note on his chest, the pencil in his hand. And by the way, that Monhegan girl was by every day you was out. I do believe she's sweet on you, Ethan Garland."

I read the note.

Read it again.

I was glad Mama had left before the words melted.

Some belong down there, others don't.

Work your seam, Ethan.

Next morning Mama came in with tea and more of the honeycake. I asked if she could find me the envelope Grandaddy'd given me the morning I went down, in more ways than one, the morning of my birthday. I was almost to the last photograph before I found it.

Him—my savior from the mine.

Down to the coal smears and the grin.

On the back, in the scrawl I knew to be Grandaddy's but clearer:

Me at fifteen. A coaldog if ever was one born.

I scanned it more closely. The face had no burn marks yet, but without question the eyes were his. They told it. Them and the grin.

Be something, they said. Something you're proud of.

For a while I lay there, trying to figure it out, getting nowhere beyond time and love; the seam holding us together, like he'd said.

Had I really seen him, really followed him out?

I was alive, wasn't I? Try and tell me different.

I dozed in fitful sleep, wakened in late afternoon to sunlight and shadow, my sisters playing somewhere. I looked out the window to see Mama had used a break in the weather to hang sheets out.

The way the wind had them dancing reminded me of kites.

Foreword to
Wind on the River

Harlan Coben

Wow.

I've been trying to come up with a unique way to say this, to express my admiration for this rich tale, to explain the wonderful hair-on-the-arms rising effect certain stories have on the reader, the ones that let you know that what you are experiencing is special, that the words will linger and stay with you and never fully leave you, that the story will rattle inside your chest and that you will be enormously grateful for that feeling. But the best I can come up with, using the vast reservoir that is my personal vocabulary (and, alas, the computer's thesaurus) is:

Wow.

Wind on the River is billed as a Christmas story. I guess that is so. But with all due respect to Richard Barre, the description is far from full. This is a love story. It is a Western. It is a tale of loyalty, of devotion, of loss and lust, of family, of quiet heroism, of redemption, of want, of healing. But I guess that would be too much to put on the cover.

Richard Barre has long been one of my favorite private-eye writers, but *Wind on the River* demonstrates what an incredible talent he is. Does it show his diversity? Yes, of course. His gift for language and storytelling? Sure. But more than that, Richard Barre's ability to move us in ways both subtle and powerful—that's what raises this story into the realm of greatness.

Greatness. I don't use that word often. But as with "Wow," it works here.

The holidays are, of course, all about tradition. Richard Barre's Christmas stories are fast becoming like well-decorated trees, stockings hung on fireplaces, candles on menorahs, exchanged presents. He has given us all a great gift with *Wind on the River.*

Cherish it.

Wind on the River

Nevada City, California
November 26, 1913

For all I knew, he came with the wind. And as I take pen to note what happened those many years ago, I close my eyes and see him still. Across time, the river mist rising to the trees, the sun I had to raise my hand against that day. As if my mind had been the very camera that took our wedding picture, Aaron's and mine, that June day at Fort Sully.

Eight years before *he* appeared...

Cheyenne River Country
Dakota Territory
December 19, 1879

As I said, there he was. Nothing but riverbend one minute, then him on that dark-maned sorrel roan of his. Like something carved and set down into my field of vision instead of the last of the potatoes I was rooting up, the occasional glance around for Mary Elizabeth clearing Jonathan's grave. Winter late in locking us in its frigid embrace, ice not yet thick enough to walk on in the Cheyenne's shallows, gravel bars poking up like the backs of sturgeon frozen where they'd breached. Bluff country this was, broken chalk tableland, the river cut acting like a funnel for the wind. The one thing Aaron hadn't taken into account when he'd set our house down where it was.

Aaron, ever the dreamer.

But I stray.

"Thought for a minute you was cavalry," the rider said as I aimed a squint up at him. No time to be alarmed, though Lord knows there was cause. Us near thirty miles from Spurlock, another hundred-plus from Fort Sully. Hawks and sky and river and rolling prairie grass bent to the wind. Aaron's idea to live out here, a concession to me, though he never said it outright.

"A cavalry soldier rooting out potatoes," I came back. "There would be a sight."

"Must have been the trousers," he said. No expression and not much more in the way of movement. Weathered tan, hat and boots showing a layer of fine white dust. "Not every day I encounter a woman in stripers."

"They'd be my husband's," I told him, hoping it might transfer some of the unease I was starting to feel now. For despite the banter, he was like none I'd seen among the farmers and merchants of Spurlock, who still expected the railroad to divert their way and make them rich. No, the closest might have been the Army scouts I'd known, hawk-eyed veterans of a thousand frontier skirmishes.

Definitely it was the eyes: faded blue, they were, with a hint of things no man and surely no woman was meant to see. Eyes that took in the barn and house soon as I mentioned Aaron, the old dugout we'd first built from sod and now used as a root cellar, the corral where a few of our mares nickered at the roan. The knoll where Mary Elizabeth had ceased her weeding and stood watching, not sure what to do, but awaiting my signal.

And what was I up to during all this looking around? Wishing I were nearer Aaron's Winchester or his New Model Army .44, both of which I took pride in knowing how to shoot. Two wolf-pelt throws and Aaron's buffalo robe testament to that.

"Your husband around?" the rider asked when his eyes had rejoined mine.

"Inside," I answered.

He weighed that. Twin Peacemakers in an oiled double holster, the butter-colored handle of something smaller protruding from his belt. Shearling coat with the collar up, gray wool trousers over the dusted boots and unroweled spurs. Tooled saddlebags, brass on the buttplate of his rifle. No farmer, yet something about him that kept my fear at bay.

Barely.

"Who's up the knoll there?" he said at length.

"My daughter."

"I meant the grave."

"My son," I told him, feeling the earth in my hands again. Hearing it hit the homemade coffin as Aaron shoveled as gently as he could to spare me, though nothing ever would. "Croup took him last winter."

"I'm sorry," he said, seeming to mean it. "How old?"

"Jonathan was seven."

The eyes left me, came back. "And your daughter?"

"Mary Elizabeth's five, thank you."

We stood there until I felt Mary Elizabeth tug at my horseblanket coat and looked down to see her sizing up the stranger.

"Hello, Mary Elizabeth," he said down to her.

"Hello." Right back, a bit like me in her directness. Something less than a virtue, often enough.

"Take the potatoes and go inside, Mary Elizabeth. Tell your father we have company."

She looked at me strangely. "But mama. Papa is—"

"*Now, Mary Elizabeth,*" I said a bit too sharply, and when she'd taken off for the house regretted.

"Papa is what?" the stranger inquired. "Besides once being a Union cavalryman and lending you his trousers."

"You are bold, aren't you?"

A gust took his reply. Something to do with time.

"My husband is in the house," I said, not altogether convincingly because of the way he regarded me. "Convalescing," I added, hoping that would stick.

The flicker in his expression passed, leaving more fatigue than curiosity. "I saw your horses," he said. "Mine's rode out. Mind if I water and feed him?"

"I suppose not."

"It wasn't meant to take advantage. I can pay."

"That won't be necessary. But we are not a rest stop. My husband and I raise horses for the fort." And whoever else will pay us for them, I thought but didn't say.

"Ma'am, we pause only of necessity," he said, dismounting gingerly. "My name is John Smith. This here's Bob Lee."

"Laney...Van Rensslaer," I said. "My husband is Aaron of the Missouri Van Rensslaers whose regiment acquitted themselves with Chamberlain and against Bloody Bill Anderson in the later stages before coming west to Forts Laramie and Sully." Too proudly, I knew, but wanting him to know who he was dealing with. You see I was anything but sure about him. Just showing up like that, miles from Spurlock and anywhere else for that matter. Wind popping like the keelboat's mainsail when it put in a week ago on its monthly stop.

"The war...yes, ma'am," he said. Letting Bob Lee make for the trough, he fumbled in a pocket, came out with a double-eagle he held out to me. "For the use of your barn. Two souls."

I hesitated. Twenty dollars.

And yet, under the circumstances...

"For Bob Lee, if not myself."

Bob Lee did look exhausted, though no more so than his rider.

"Two souls," I agreed, palming the gold piece after an appropriate pause.

We saw no more of either of them that day.

December 20, 1879

As it was Sunday, we spent the morning reading the Bible around Aaron's bed after I'd fed and bathed him. In the spirit, I'd had Mary Elizabeth put a portion of our breakfast inside the barn door. Nothing fancy, biscuits and gravy, a few pennies measured against the double eagle. I was reading Luke 15:11-32, the Prodigal, when I heard the floorboards creak, and there stood John Smith, my empty plate in his hand. Too amazed to address this presumption, I merely sat as his eyes took in Aaron, Mary Elizabeth in her Sunday dress, me in mine.

Then the doorway was empty.

When we'd regained ourselves and changed clothes, we heard an axe. I bade Mary Elizabeth continue her Bible reading, such as she'd been able to master, which was quite accomplished for age five, if I say so myself, then went outside to find him by the shed. Shirt off, a strong sun for little more than freezing beating down on his back. Already he'd blocked out about a quarter of a cord. Sweat ran from his hair and glistened on his skin. Propped against the side of the barn was his rifle and, over a post, his double holster.

For a moment I watched, then I said, "At this house, we observe the Lord's day, Mr. Smith."

He spoke as if knowing I'd been there all the time, though I was quiet in my approach. "And his son wasn't born in the Dakotas, Mrs. Van Rensslaer. I doubt he expects the same adherence this time of year."

I felt a flush rise. "You're very—"

"Bold. I know." *Chop.*

"Mary Elizabeth and I can stack that tomorrow."

"Thank you for the breakfast," he said, splitting another log.

"The least I could do for what it bought."

Not knowing whether to get back to Mary Elizabeth or attempt further intercession on behalf of the Lord, I compromised. "Bob Lee need salt lick or liniment?"

Chop. "Other than a romp with those mares of yours, Bob Lee's about as happy as he's been for a while."

"Then I expect you'll be moving on."

"I will at that, Mrs. Van Rensslaer."

"And may I ask where you're headed?"

"You may." *Chop.*

I waited, as he picked up another log and positioned it, but no destination was offered. Finally he said, "Why's your husband like that?"

"As I mentioned, my husband is convalescing," I answered coolly. "Mornings he spends in bed."

Chop.

"You folks know what you're doing out here?"

"I'm sure I don't know what you mean, Mr. Smith. And I'll have your respect when you address me."

"Believe me, it's yours, ma'am. How long has he been like that?"

"My affair, if it's all the same to you."

I'd turned and was making for the house when he said, "A girl of five and a husband who stares at the ceiling?"

"Mary Elizabeth is almost six and of great help. And now we'll thank you to be on your way."

He brought the axe down, left the blade angled in the block. He'd picked up his shirt and guns and was making for the barn when I felt Mary Elizabeth's scream like an arrow.

The knife Mary Elizabeth had been using to etch holly and letters into a split and flattened lard can was an apple corer I hadn't seen in years. Somehow she'd dug it up and nearly severed three of her fingers with it. The blood had to be as terrifying as the pain because there she was when I threw back the door, bouncing around the kitchen, smearing everything she touched.

"*It was for you*," she kept wailing. "*For Christmas. Ow, ow, ow, ow, ow.*"

"Mary Elizabeth, look at me, you're all right," I tried to distract her. But she was impossible to hold and less so to convince, wild and slippery. That is until John Smith caught and held her to him.

"You need to stop the bleeding," he said, gripping her wrist as blood poured off the hand. Wrapping it in his shirt while she moaned, her eyes wide with fear.

With the pressure John Smith applied, the bleeding slowed, and I got after needle and thread. Finally I made the eye and went to work, my child screaming with each new jab. I was making a mess of it, losing my grip and feeling each inept stitch myself, cursing her struggles, when in a steady voice he bade us switch. I protested, I'm sure I did. But her hysteria settled it and I relinquished the needle and set about calming her.

To my amazement the stitching was done then and he directed me to wrap it, which I did, though blood persisted in places. For a while we just sat, Mary Elizabeth keening and John Smith telling her how brave she'd been and how he'd seen grown men cry out far worse for their mamas. Finally the whiskey and milk and honey took hold and she nodded off.

As he laid her in bed, I elevated her bandaged hand on pillows. "Thank you," I told him.

"I'd clean it every day, not to tell you your business."

"May I ask where you acquired such a skill?"

"Man picks up what he picks up," was all he answered. Which was fine by me, nothing wrong with not filling the air with words. Women did enough of that, heaven knew, especially town women. But after I'd set to in the kitchen with towels and water, John Smith nodded at our bedroom, Aaron's and mine, and said, "He doesn't hear, either?"

"Not in the usual sense."

"What did it?"

Not quite sure why, I told him. How Aaron, while in town on one of his infrequent trips, had been goaded into a fight. How one of the men who beat him finished it with a pick handle. How Aaron had made no sound since, Doc Stroebel, when he brought Aaron back, merely shaking his head and telling me to keep him comfortable. That he could slip away or come out of it, there was no way of telling. About the guilt I felt when it got to be too much and I'd have to go down to the river and scream, the wind taking it like the wolf calls we heard on moonlit nights.

All of it pouring out like the Cheyenne in flood.

"How is it he sustains life?" John Smith asked.

"He'll swallow what I put up to him. That reflex still works." As does what comes with it, I thought but didn't add.

"And you've managed out here?"

"The horses even out. Aaron's pension helps."

"Ever think of moving to town?"

"We quite like it here, thank you," I said, too rapidly.

For a while John Smith said nothing. Then, "What are you, Mrs. Van Rensslaer, twenty-four?"

"Twenty-six. What difference does that make?"

"Hard not to notice how much closer you are to my age than his."

Anger flared in me. "I will tolerate no such talk of my husband. Aaron saved me from something far worse than death, if you know anything of loneliness and melancholy. He is the kindest man I ever knew."

He finished his coffee and, almost as an afterthought, said, "The fight was over you, wasn't it?"

I nearly dropped my cup.

"No joy being an outcast among your own people, is it?"

He stood, Mary Elizabeth's blood close to set on his shirt. "The tattoo on your neck," he added. "Sioux or Northern Cheyenne, if I had to guess." Then, glancing out at the river, "Bob Lee and I are much obliged for the hospitality. We can still make time."

He was almost to the door when I blurted, "Mr. Smith, wait. At least let me soak out your shirt." Despite my flareup and subsequent astonishment, feeling more than beholden for his assistance. "Aaron has one you can put on while it dries. Meantime, I'll start supper. That way you can start fresh at daylight."

From the way he stiffened I thought my words had fallen on deaf ears. Until I realized that something out the window had brought him up short. Without turning from it he said, "You really want to help, go to the barn and unsaddle Bob Lee. Pile hay over the saddle and turn him out among your mares. You can tell them you traded one of yours for him. That I lit out west."

"Why would I do that? Tell who?"

"Them," he said, pointing to the column of dust.

Barely had I finished when their horses topped the rise and plunged into the river, arriving in my yard still dripping. Twenty-five or -six of them, fanning out around the leader. Some were in dusters as he was, others in wool or leather coats, all with pistols on their hips. The leader, who was wearing close-fitting black gloves, was a florid-faced man of perhaps forty. Finished with his initial visual survey, he tipped his hat to me and said, "Mrs. Van Rensslaer?"

"And you would be?" I answered, trying to stay calm.

"Captain William Longstreet. You might have heard of our agency. The Pinkerton?"

"I have indeed," I responded with more confidence than I felt.

"We're gratified to hear it."

The warmth had fled from the day, leaving the sky tasseled with high white streaks. Standing in the thin light, wishing for my horseblanket, I said, "You'd be the bunch still after the James gang. Lest you caught up the last couple of weeks and the news is late arriving."

They exchanged looks, and I wondered if I hadn't picked too hard at a scab. Eight years and neither Frank nor Jesse in jail, a fact I knew from the keelboat people.

"A matter of time, ma'am," Longstreet assured me. "The Younger contingent is another story. After the failed raid at Northfield, Minnesota, Cole, Bob, and Jim now get their mail in Stillwater pen." He paused to eye the barn again. "But the Youngers are not the reason for this call. Their cousin would be, a murderous killer as ever drew breath. One Jubal Pyne." He spat in the dust. "Not only was he with them at Northfield, three weeks ago he accounted for two of the finest lawmen to wear the badge. Agents Vogel and Pennington, gunned down outside Independence."

"Independence being Missouri."

"Yes, ma'am, and only adding to his total. Recently he was spotted at Fort Pierre. Which would follow because he uses rivers to cover his tracks. We believe that to include the Missouri and now the Cheyenne."

I'd become conscious of one of his lieutenants taking my measure unashamedly. Before I knew it, I'd put a hand to my throat and as quickly removed it.

"And you believe him here?"

"People in Spurlock said you lived along the river. We were hoping you might have seen him." He handed me an illustrated wanted poster and I tried not to gasp. Because there he was, the man in my house, the man I knew as John Smith.

Jubal Pyne.

It even described Bob Lee.

An agent who'd been eyeing the corral eased his horse over, whispered something to Longstreet, and I knew from his look that what I said next was crucial.

"Big as life," I told him, handing it back. "Sold him a mare—forty dollars plus the one he was riding. The roan over there, dark mane? That would be his."

There was a stir among the mounted agents, several edging closer to the barn. Longstreet raised his hand for quiet and, failing to mask the gleam in his eye, asked me when Jubal Pyne had shown himself.

I hesitated, as if in thought, which was every bit the truth.

"Week or more ago," I answered then. "Just came, did his business and left."

"You get a gander at which way?"

"Let me think. West, I believe. Along the river."

"Then you don't mind if we search the barn and the house?"

Though it sent a chill through me, I'd anticipated it and answered, "I'll take you inside. My daughter badly cut herself this afternoon and my husband is also resting."

"Thank you, but we'll handle it. Man like that, you can't be too careful."

They were going to regardless, I knew, so I allowed it, all the while asking myself what in hell I was doing. The risk if it turned bad. But scrutinizing Longstreet and his agents gave me no assurance that Jubal Pyne would return alive in their care, and no matter what he'd done, every man deserved a chance. Then there was Mary Elizabeth. No cold-blooded killer would have held her that way, reassuring when under the circumstances he could have taken what he fancied and left us imperiled.

The man beside Longstreet motioned and two groups peeled off, one toward the house, the other toward the barn and dugout, Longstreet saying, "Our sympathies regarding your husband, ma'am. We learned of his misfortune."

But I was not so easily distracted. "Please tell your men that everything gets left as it is," I replied. "Water and hay, all you want, but three mouths live here."

"You heard the lady," Longstreet called out. "As is."

For the first time, the man beside him spoke, the one who had been appraising me. "That why you live so far out, ma'am? Spurlock not what you'd call partial to white squaws?"

"Who is this man," I demanded of Longstreet.

"Agent Zel Clausen, late of Clay County, Missouri," he said with a glance that might or might not have been judgmental. "Knows Jesse and Frank by sight, he does. Jubal Pyne, as well."

Clausen tipped his hat. "That I do. *Ma'am.*"

"Well, agent Clausen will keep a civil tongue in his head or he will leave this property," I said, my flush no act. "A person's preference for domicile is no concern of his."

Clausen added a smile to his list of sins. "Fact is, I've heard them bucks can smell a white woman ten miles off. You find that true in your experience?"

A snicker went up from the remaining posse. Over the rushing in my ears, I could hear the wind rattling my corn, the fan blades turning above the trough. Finally I bit down and said something like, "Climb down off that horse, Agent Clausen, and see how much you have left to imagine with when I'm done with you."

The smile became an evil grin. "Might just take you up on that—*ma'am.*" Looking around for support among his cohorts and, sad to say, finding some.

"That will be enough," Longstreet said, halting the murmur. And to me, "Manners tend not to accompany long rides. They mean no harm."

By now the other agents were back and mounting up, shaking their heads at Longstreet. One came licking sweet potato pie off his fingers. Which ordinarily would have set me off, but in light of Clausen's remark I was able to put in perspective. It also gave me a chance to simmer down and remember what was at stake.

"That said, my offer for hay and water still stands," I told him.

"Much obliged, but I doubt our quarry will be feeding and watering with daylight left." He reined his horse, clucked to it. "Good luck to you this winter, ma'am. And don't worry about the Jubal Pyne's of this world, they're finished. They just don't know it yet."

With a final leer from Clausen, Longstreet led them out of the yard and across the river.

I remember watching their dust plume over the willows.

The Pinkertons had given Aaron the berth they might a crazed person. Which made Jubal Pyne's decision to take refuge under Aaron's bed a clever one. Yet it troubled me that he'd put Aaron in harm's way, and I told him so in no uncertain terms.

I could see him struggle with the challenge. Finally he said, "I figured the chance of any shooting was lessened by it, ma'am. If I chose wrong, I own up to it."

"Wrong would appear to be your side in more than this instance."

We were at the kitchen table, darkness close about the log house. Mary Elizabeth still sleeping after her ordeal and Jubal Pyne taking frequent peeks at the moonlit river, thinking the Pinkertons could have double-backed a watch, despite my having seen nothing to suggest it.

"Peaceful out here," he said after one such lookout.

"Used to be," I answered.

He broke off a piece of bread and chewed it. "You don't know them, what they're capable of."

"And what are you capable of, *Jubal Pyne?*"

He swallowed. "Like anyone, I suppose I'm finding out."

"Anyone didn't kill Longstreet's agents."

In the silence I could hear the wicks burning in the kerosene lamps, the wind tapping my leafless bushes against the glass.

"Did you?" I asked him directly. "Kill those men?"

"I did, ma'am."

"And you saw fit to bring that into my house."

A weariness seemed to take him. He regarded hands one might assume belonged to a pianist or doctor, not a gunfighter. "I had no idea they were as near or I'd have ridden on. Bob Lee and I will be gone before sunup. With apologies, if you'll have them."

"I'll have them," I said. "Also an explanation, which I feel is no more than I am due."

"Don't assume to be alone in that," he said after a pause.

The rest of the evening, the cold supper we shared, the chores afterward, we spent in silence.

After feeding Aaron, checking on Mary Elizabeth, I lay awake listening to the wind. Hearing in it *Don't assume to be alone in that* and wondering at his meaning, at the choices he'd made. Two men he'd shot down. *Only adding to his total*, Longstreet made sure to mention. Yet Jubal Pyne was not the man he described. To cite evidence, there was his way with Mary Elizabeth...his speech...his manner with me. They did not reflect Longstreet's words. As if one fallen through ice and pounding for release could only appear distorted to those on the other side.

I yearned for sleep, but none came.

The excitement, I told myself.

At length I got up and looked in on Mary Elizabeth. She'd tangled in the covers, so I readjusted them, careful of her hand. I kissed her forehead, which at least felt warm despite the cold that had crept in. Thinking some leftover tapioca would help, I had some of that. But I was stalling, I knew, and after drying my hands, I put on boots and the horseblanket over my nightshift and went out to the barn.

Holding the lantern high, I searched for him and spotted Bob Lee in the stall next to our milk cow and the chicken coop. The area where our other horses would be when the ice set in.

"Mr. Pyne," I called quietly, hoping he would be asleep so that I could go back in and end this foolishness. To my right, I saw his bedroll well back in the straw, but not him.

Then a shadow moved.

"Are you alone?" he asked.

"I am."

I heard the sound of a hammer standing down, the creak of leather. Stepping into the light, he said, "Something you need?"

I took a breath, hung the lantern on a peg, caught the milk cow's placid gaze. "For one thing," I said, "you could do me the favor of accepting my apology. You are a guest in my home, and I was rude."

"You came to tell me that?"

"It needed saying. I didn't want to miss you in the morning."

He came closer, so that I was looking directly up at him. "You'll catch your death," he said.

"I'm hardly as frail as that, Mr. Pyne." I was about to add something like *much as I've seen on these plains*, but before I knew it his fingers were brushing aside the hair at my neck.

Instead of recoiling as I should have, I merely covered the tattoo.

"You mentioned respect," he said. "Try fortitude. Anyone who makes it away from the Northern Cheyenne owns it and more." And to my look, "I heard Clausen. He's a bad one, by the way."

I could say nothing, just clutch my coat tighter about me.

"You want to talk about it?" he asked.

"It wasn't Cheyenne, it was Oglala Sioux," I told him as we sat on hay bales, the light between us, his eyes on mine. "Three days from Fort Laramie they waited for our wagons. My whole family fell. We always said we'd kill ourselves, but when the time came, I could not. I lived because they liked blonde hair."

Barely conscious I was twisting a braid, a childhood habit.

"Three years I was with them, and though the beatings accorded a slave were hard, no buck ever touched me the way Clausen said."

"You survived," Jubal Pyne said. "Clausen wouldn't have."

"The tattoo denotes ownership. There'd have been more, but I pretended to faint. One day in fall, a United States soldier rode in to discuss a treaty detail. Though I was herded inside, Aaron saw me and made them an offer. As we left, him poorer by his saddle and me behind him on his mount, I kept expecting the arrows. I still expect them."

He said nothing.

"It took months to come all the way back, but a year later at Fort Sully we were married. Aaron took retirement and we moved out here." To which I added, "After too long in Spurlock."

His nod held more understanding than words.

"Mary Elizabeth keeps asking if he'll play with her again."

"What do you tell her?"

"That maybe God is waiting for Christmas."

He said, "Hope got you this far, Mrs. Van Rensslaer. Don't give it up."

"No? What about you?"

He broke off a piece of hay and chewed it. "I believe there's another side to all this and that I have to find it. That maybe it's not someplace but someone."

"I have to go," I said. "Aaron gets chilled." I'd stood and was reaching for the lamp, feeling not a little lightheaded, when something made me ask, "*Were* you at Northfield?"

"I was not."

"But Longstreet said—"

"Grudges die hard in Missouri. I was at Centralia when two hundred bluecoats died, twenty-five of them unarmed."

I gasped. "You rode with Bloody Bill Anderson? Against my husband?"

"You never heard of Order Number 11? Families like mine who sympathized with the South burned out or murdered? Tell it to my wife, she was carrying our son. Why do you think there *are* Jameses and Youngers?"

"I don't know. Do you?"

He rubbed his eyes. "I was eighteen at Centralia. They had me patching up the wounded. That ended it for me."

"Then why are you here?"

"Clausen's brother died there. When he signed on with the Pinkertons, my name made Longstreet's list. Liberty, Gads Hill, Blue Cut—every robbery within three states, he had me there."

"And Independence?"

"Two of them waited for me at a livery" he said. "No warning, just that wanted poster."

"I believe I've heard enough for one day and night, thank you."

"Laney, listen to me, I don't have time to not say it. Stay tonight."

I was stunned into silence.

"Aaron's better off where they can care for him, you know that. We can make a life in Montana. California, if you want."

"Given what Aaron's meant to me, I'll pretend I didn't hear that."

"Pretend all you want," he said. "But I'm not sure I can find you a second time."

I wasn't sure the flush had risen to my face, but I wasn't taking any chances. In haste I said, "My husband needs me, Mr. Pyne. I'll have breakfast and something for the trail at five."

And with that I hurried back inside my cold house.

December 21, 1879

The unseasonable weather ended that day. Morning saw the clouds thicken and by noon we had three inches of snow with more likely. I'd risen at four and had eggs and potatoes and leftover biscuits ready when Jubal Pyne knocked. Our conversation was sparse, as if what was said the night before was a dust devil that had moved on. When he finished eating, I watched him check on Mary Elizabeth then lead Bob Lee from the barn and head west.

Part of me left with him, for reasons I did not fully understand. But, of course, I did. Other than Aaron, no man had spoken to me that way, let alone triggered the feelings I had watching him go. Can one be punished for thoughts, I kept wondering, for feelings not rigorously suppressed? I was afraid of the answer.

To keep my mind where it belonged, I set to my chores, among them washing the towels we'd used tending to Mary Elizabeth. Without her help things went slowly. I was through with the wash, hanging it in the barn, when I felt a presence behind me and turned to face the proverbial arrow.

Clausen grinned. "Your kid said you might be out here."

In the dim quiet I could hear his breathing.

"You were in the house?" I said, as much incredulous as fearful.

He slapped snow off his hat, tossed it aside. "Bothers you, huh? Woman good looking as you ought to think about locks."

"What are you doing here?"

"That's for me to know and you to find out. You can start by taking off those clothes."

I looked beyond him to the door. "Where's Captain Longstreet?"

"Far enough to be of use to me and none to you. Now are you going to get to it or do I start in on your girl and that old man?"

Time...time and guilt.

"This how you repay the Pinkertons' faith in you?"

"Three dead and your place in ashes," he said, shedding his coat. Unbuckling his gunbelt and letting it drop. "How long before they think your savages done it?"

My savages.

I was close enough to grab the hook from a bale and hold it in a threatening manner. By God, I would not go down without a fight.

"Fine by me," he said, grinning. "You want it hard, we do it hard."

I was agile enough to wing him to no effect before he twisted the hook and leveled me with a blow. Through stars I felt him tugging at Aaron's pants, his hardness on my leg, my shirt buttons giving way. Then his hand was inside, squeezing me until I cried out.

That was the last of him I felt.

There seemed to be two Clausens, one wrenched backward in a gloved hand. Whoever it was had him by the hair, and as I watched, drove his face into a post. Again then, and I could hear his nose break, his roar of pain as the gloved fist struck it twice more.

But Clausen wasn't done.

Pulling a knife from his boot, slashing the air with it, he backed the other off and dove for his fallen holster.

That was when Jubal Pyne drew as fast as I'd ever seen and fired.

For a long time he held me as I shook. I could feel the strength of him, the solidity, his breath in my hair as he stroked it. My face in his hands as I lost myself in the tobacco and talc and leather of him.

Rough stubble and the smell of hay.

The wind in the loft.

Finally Jubal Pyne let out a breath.

"You all right?" he asked, as though hesitant to speak.

"I'm not sure," I said, equally so. "Ask me another time."

He just nodded.

"Turn your head, please. Is Clausen dead?"

"He is."

"How—?"

"I saw him headed this way and tailed him. Bastard never even looked around."

But already my mind was a locomotive. "Longstreet valued him," I said. "He'll follow his tracks."

"The general direction, he will. But enough snow fell to cover the final miles."

The snow that now had stopped.

"Which means they'll be coming," I said.

"Which means I have work to do."

It made sense what Jubal Pyne said about disposing of him in the open; spaded snow stuck out like a crypt and the river was too low and sluggish to take a body far. Which eased my mind not at all when he buried him in the mass stall and let mares into it along with their green manure and some dried, then worked them up enough to hoof down the bulge and make it look innocent.

Three o'clock, Longstreet rode in with a crew of six.

"Looking for a man," he said. Bob Lee turned out again, Jubal Pyne somewhere in the loft with his rifle. "You remember Clausen?"

A flight of late geese honked on their way south.

"Well enough," I answered, wishing I were with them.

"Tracks indicated he might have followed through on some things he told one of us last night. Whiskey talk, till he didn't turn up at muster."

"Haven't seen the man," I said. "No great loss to me."

His breath hung in the air. "Clausen's hewn rough, ma'am, but he knows his work."

"Not for a minute do I doubt it."

"You haven't seen him, then?"

"Trust me that I'd know, Captain."

His eyes swept the house, the barn and dugout, came to rest on the outhouse. "Any objection to our using the facility?"

"None at all," I told him, knowing he was testing me. "Long as you're gentlemen about it."

"Anybody?" he offered his men. Nodding to one in particular who got down and made his way there, drawing his pistol and holding it to his thigh before entering. Once back, exchanging looks with Longstreet, who said, "Guess we'll be going, ma'am. Your husband doing better?"

"Well as can be expected," I answered.

"Glad of it. You, too, I hope."

It caught me by surprise, too long before recognition dawned: the bruise where Clausen almost knocked me cold.

"Corral gate," I covered. "Running off a coyote."

The windmill clattered in a gust.

"Liniment's useful for swelling," he said after a look. He was turning away when he added, "By the way, I know some who'd give you a fair price for that mount of Pyne's."

"Thanks, I'll keep it in mind." Regaining my breath only when they'd scattered the ice reaching for the river's middle and crested the far bank.

***

I was relating my exchange with Longstreet, Jubal Pyne listening without comment, when Mary Elizabeth appeared in her nightgown and held out her bandage.

Her bandage. In all that had happened, I'd forgotten to change it.

"Mama it hurts. A really lot."

"I know sweetheart," I said. "You're mama's brave girl."

"Then you're not mad at me?"

"How could I be mad at you for making me a present?"

"Mr. Smith isn't mad I didn't make him one?"

"Mr. Smith is just glad to see you on your feet," he told her.

"Papa is too," she answered brightly. "He told me so."

A chill gripped me. Aaron, to my knowledge, was the same as he'd been since July, neither a wave of the hand nor a syllable. Trying to keep the urgency from my voice, I said, "Papa told you this? When?"

"Just now, when he told me to show you my hand."

I checked Aaron: no change. Around my heart in my mouth, I said, "Come here," and felt Mary Elizabeth's cheek.

The skin was as warm as her hand was swollen.

After I'd set her hand in warm water, iodine, and Epsom salts, I sat staring at the snow falling outside while Jubal Pyne made coffee. Handing me mine, he said, "If you're blaming yourself, don't. It was the blade. I've seen enough to know."

"And?"

"I won't lie to you about blood poisoning."

"Lord help us. Are you sure?"

"You saw the line starting up her wrist?"

Tears welled. I felt his hand on mine and in my state left it there.

"It's early," he said. "I've seen the salts work, too."

I searched his eyes. "When can you tell?"

"Morning, I expect."

* * *

We passed the night in shifts, Jubal Pyne insisting I rest, perhaps seeing a line rising in me, too, each of us trying to keep Mary Elizabeth's hand in the solution. Which was a hard row as restless as she was, whimpering in fevered sleep. As for me, I slept not at all during the shifts that were his, just lay in bed praying and mulling over thoughts of remorse and penance.

Tick-tock intruded the clock on the mantel.

Normally my ally in sleep, it now only made the night longer.

Toward morning, Mary Elizabeth sat up and asked, "Will he be hungry?"

"Who'll be hungry, sweetheart?"

"Papa when he wakes up."

"No sweetheart, he'll be fine," I told her. "That's why we feed him."

"I'm glad, mama."

"I'm glad you're glad."

"Mama?" Her brown eyes beseeching mine from under the cloth I'd laid on her forehead to cool it. "Please make it stop hurting."

December 22, 1879

By mid-morning the sky was the mottle of tarnished silver. Snow lay against the barn and had nearly obliterated the sod dugout. I'd just finished feeding Aaron his potato soup, reading to him afterward, my mind on Mary Elizabeth, when I sensed Jubal Pyne standing where I'd first seen him in the house, in Aaron's doorway. Now it would have been unexpected had he *not* been there.

I said, "You're wondering why I read to him, aren't you?"

"Have to say it crossed my mind," he answered.

"He can hear me, I know he can. It's what I meant by not in the usual sense."

A moment went by. Then, "Any objection if I smoke?"

I shook my head and he lit a cigarette he'd already rolled.

"One thing I do know," he said, exhaling. "If Aaron can hear you, anyone can."

Tired as I was and in no mood to opine who'd been receiving my prayers of late, which I assumed was his point, I said nothing. A moment went by as he focused on Aaron's face, the book in my hands.

"You get any rest?"

"Enough," I said.

Wind howled down the chimney and around the sashes.

"I hope so," he said.

Jubal Pyne looked up from the wood, which hissed and popped where he'd laid it. Yet beyond the fire's radius, the cold prevailed with a vengeance, Aaron's hot water bottles lasting only short intervals before needing filling again.

"Line's risen a good inch since last night," he said regarding Mary Elizabeth, visible through her open door. "No news to you."

I assured him I had eyes, thank you.

"Laney, there's only so much we can do here. She needs a doctor."

"It's early, you said so yourself."

His expression remained unchanged.

"Long as you're on what's needed, a break in the storm would be nice," I snapped. Then, after a breath, "Sorry. I'd be obliged if you'd hitch up the wagon so I can take her in."

"Wagon won't make it without a road to follow."

I said, "Then I'll saddle one of the mares."

"Thirty miles. In ice and snow." And when I'd not responded, "Bob Lee and I stand the best chance."

From the way he said it, the only chance.

"You forgetting the Pinkertons?" I asked. "Where they're likely holed up in this?"

"You see them catch me so far?"

"I'll ride Bob Lee."

"He's too much horse. He's not used to you."

"In a few miles he will be."

"You won't make it. Which means the three of you."

Taking a breath, having admitted this to no one—and I mean *no* one—I said, "I lost a son waiting too long. Do you think I'd risk my daughter by—" I had to stop and compose myself.

"I'm going. You're not. That's it."

"And what of Aaron?" he said.

"Feed him every four hours. Keep him warm."

"You'd trust your husband to me after—"

"Yes," I said, looking him square in the eye.

He hunched over to light another cigarette. When he rose up his face had hardened into the one I'd first seen aboard Bob Lee.

"I lied to you," he said. "Every bank and train Longstreet has me up for I was there. I've killed more men than you can count. You think I'd let one more stand in my way?"

"I'll be saddling the gray," I said. "Wrap Elizabeth for me, will you?"

Throwing the cigarette in the fire, he took a Peacemaker from its holster and started for Aaron's room. He had a pillow over Aaron's face, the barrel to it and the hammer back, when I screamed, *"No! Don't!"*

"Watch me. Better yet, give me a reason."

"You can't." And before I knew it, *"I love you."*

"Then you're a bigger fool than I thought. Take off the blinders, a man like me only wants one thing from a woman."

By then I could hardly see.

"You're not like that. You had a wife. You had children."

"That was a kid I served with who died. Once a thief, right?" His grin was a blade. "There, you all right *now*? As I recall, you wanted me to ask."

I could only stand there.

"You can do better than that, Mrs. Van Rensslaer. Speak up."

"I hate you," I said.

"Say it again."

"I hate you."

For a moment that seemed like forever, I could hear my heart pounding. Later, as Bob Lee left the barn and headed toward the river, Mary Elizabeth a mere bulge inside Jubal Pyne's coat, I allowed myself a look. But only then.

* * *

December 25, 1879

The days before Christmas were a blur. Snow fell on and off, the temperature as if there were no bottom. Christmas Eve, I crawled in beside Aaron and held him, and in the process warmed us both enough to give the water bottles a rest. I even thought he moved a little. Finally the 25th dawned as if the weather meant the day to be a gift: calm and bright.

I'd shoveled my way to the barn and was milking the cow around midday when I heard a hail and went outside to find Doc Stroebel in his rig, the most welcome sight beside him on the seat.

"*Mama*," Mary Elizabeth said, getting down and wading toward me. "*I'm back.*" And as I picked her up and held her, being careful of her new bandage, "Why are you crying? I'm fine now."

As she skipped toward the house, Doc handed me a box with a roast dinner his wife had fixed us. Saying to my thanks, "Men I know will be here tomorrow to chop wood and such, whatever you need. And the man who paid for Mary Elizabeth wanted you to have this."

The sack held more double-eagles than I'd seen all year.

I was afraid to ask, but I did. "This man, he get away all right?"

"Course not, you wouldn't have heard. Pinkertons gunned him, recognized his horse outside the saloon. Some big outlaw they'd been chasing." And with a look at me over his spectacles, "If you can picture an outlaw going in to get drunk in a town full of Pinkertons. After delivering what he did."

Ice ran in my veins. I could neither move nor speak.

Doc touched my arm. "Figured you had enough on your plate without me volunteering to them why he'd come, and from where."

Then, with a look at the house, Mary Elizabeth bounding about, "A gift is only a gift when you accept it, Laney. Don't make it less."

"Doc, I—"

"Change her dressing often, there's ointment in the box. Oh, and that Pinkerton on his way out of town asked me to give you this." Reaching into a pocket for it. "Said you'd know what it meant."

Folded into the wanted poster were bank notes and a sheet with handwriting I decided to read: *One sorrel roan in the amount of $100, freely transacted this day of our Lord, 25 December 1879.* Underlined was, *No further consideration required.*

It was signed William Longstreet.

After Doc checked Aaron he was anxious to get back, so I thanked him again for Mary Elizabeth and the food and all, then watched until his rig was a black speck against the snow. Out there beyond the river.

Until the wind picked up and I went inside.

Aaron rallied that spring, but he was never the same. And yet, we were happy. After a trip that's another story, we made it to California, where we got into the laundry business, then the hotel business, our own before he died. Mary Elizabeth is a doctor in Salt Lake and our son Jubal was just made an adjutant under General Pershing at the Presidio.

Still, despite our turn of fortune, the white cloths and the silver and the crystal, I now and then take out the double eagle I refused to spend even when things got tight.

And I hold it. And I hear the wind again.

The way it gets inside a person and won't come out.

Foreword to
The Shepherd

Brad Parks

I'll always remember Lowlife Louie.

When I met him, I was a cub reporter for *The Star-Ledger* (Newark, N.J.). He was a member of a minor-league professional wrestling promotion that had sprung up in nearby Bayonne and was attracting fans by offering something televised wrestling did not: real violence.

One Friday night a month, he and his buddies were slicing themselves with razor blades, scraping themselves with cheese graters, gouging themselves with barbed wire, spilling buckets of blood in the name of entertainment.

"I could be bleeding with a guy who has AIDS," Lowlife Louie told me. "They don't check for that. I really don't care."

It was a bad scene, made worse because unsuspecting families were showing up at these events, thinking they were going to get the kind of theatrical, sanitized professional wrestling the WWF gave them. Instead, their five-year-olds were getting hit with blood spatter in the second row.

I wrote a feature about it that landed on the front page of the Sunday paper. The next day, New Jersey Governor Christie Whitman announced legislation to ban Lowlife Louie and his buddies, or at least to assure young kids weren't exposed to them.

Perhaps this is all just prelude to saying: Yes, I'm a sucker for reporter-as-hero stories.

Especially when it's a young reporter, like Gabe Vasconsalles, the protagonist of this gripping, expertly crafted story from Richard Barre.

There's just no feeling like being a young newspaper reporter. As with a lot of young people, you are outraged by the world's injustices. The difference is, you feel you can actually do something about the situation. You've got this vehicle, the newspaper, and you ride around feeling the power of its engine rumbling under your legs and in your soul.

I can't pretend that tackling a small-time wrestling promotion compares to the evil Gabe faces in this story. But I can testify that Barre captures the *mise-en-scène* of the young reporter with remarkable clarity.

He also nails newspapers, Los Angeles in the late 50s, sex, drugs, race, aging and, of course, the at-times-brutish thuggery of the human condition. It would be a remarkable accomplishment for a 100,000-word novel. That he achieves it in a 5,700-word story is breathtaking. That he does so with a compelling voice and such beautiful imagery is nothing short of humbling to those of us who also fancy ourselves writers.

Luckily, as a reader, you don't have to worry about being humbled. All you have to do is sit back, give yourself over to the ride, and enjoy a master at work.

The Shepherd

Me? I came out from Pueblo that summer, looking less ahead than over my shoulder. Greyhound or no, any minute expecting a final threat or insult to reach across the sage and jackrabbits and nail me in the ear. The fighting Vasconsallii, my memory of them dulled by boot camp soon as my old man could sign the papers. Two years in Hamburg, two more in Carolina...Elvis getting inducted about the only thing stirring up the troops that year. That is, until I got home in October and rejoined the family front.

One endless skirmish—worse than battle.

At least in battle you lived apart from the enemy.

Knock it off, I told myself. It was like surviving a bombardment only to keep hearing it. Artillery growing louder with the distance.

The bus passed a doorless flatbed, its occupants waving away the fat diesel fumes. Finally I took my own advice.

I turned around and kept my eyes forward.

That was the year Mickey and Duke and I found new homes. Duke's at Memorial Coliseum with Gil Hodges and Charlie Neal, that short leftfield fence. Mickey's at a magic kingdom with Minnie, Donald and a million wide-eyed angels. Mine in the City of Hardened Angels with Dodge and Carston, Rose DeChampagne and the rest.

Nineteen fifty-eight, it was.

The year of The Shepherd.

A guy at the bus depot who looked like he might understand such things suggested the place. And I actually walked to it, seventeen blocks. That's how young I was then.

Twenty-two...imagine that.

Los Angeles, to its credit, put on no pretense. None of that tourist-poster stuff—just here it is, right between the eyes. Ninety degrees when we rolled in, sun-squint off a million windows, smog all the talk in the paper I copped off a bus bench. After seventeen blocks, the pavement coming through my shoes like a flame thrower.

And then...there it was. THE SHEPHERD running down the Hope Street side in one of those long-stemmed vertical Ls braced to the building. HOTEL in smaller letters on the horizontal.

I remember thinking it might have been something at one time, that maybe the neighborhood was dragging it down, the whole area looking burnt-out and laid-over. Then I concluded the lean was mutual—exhausted boxers holding each other up. The hotel was on the southeast corner: seven floors of brick and once-light concrete, once-black ironwork bleeding rust, once-outward windows cataracted by grime and yellowing pull-downs. Corner tiles looking antiqued from the grit. Swirly, bannery thing reading 1920 surrounded by a grouping of stained-faced cherubs peering down from the eaves.

At least the lobby was empty and dim away from the plate glass and fading drapes. Frayed couches and overstuffed chairs, anemic palm tree, a framed watercolor of sand dunes. Dust peppered my nose as I stepped to the front desk, the signs behind it blurting RENT PAYABLE BY CHECK OR MONEY ORDER. NO CASH ACCEPTED. VISITORS 8AM TO 4PM—LOBBY ONLY.

"Help you?" a voice asked when I'd finished sneezing.

He was beefy and black, his face framed by the cut-out in the glass. Wiry short hair graying at the temples, flared nostrils, once-bad skin that might have profited by a beard.

"Heard you rent by the month," I said, wiping my eyes.

He nodded. "One-twenty—in advance. Otherwise it's six-fifty a night."

Behind him the sweep hand of a wall clock seemed to shift into low as it passed six and labored toward the twelve.

"I was told eighty-five."

"By who, Father Time? Got a sink in the room, radiator, bath at opposite ends of the hall. Linen once a week. You put it on."

Goodbye Pueblo, I thought. "It's really more than I—"

"Taking or leaving?"

"Taking," I said after shifting my feet, burning up in my Payless oxfords. "Traveler's checks all right?"

"Long as they ain't stolen."

He watched as I signed them, slid them under the glass at him, his eyes narrowing to read the name.

"Vasconsalles," I clarified. "Gabriel."

"With a red brushcut and freckles?"

"Looks that way."

"Wetback?"

"Nope." Guessing what my old man would have done with that one—even money on him despite the hundred pounds he'd give the guy. Four decades of high-plains winters, bare-knuckle boxing matches when he wasn't out being a human tractor.

"Kiddin' with you," the man said. "But a word to the wise, no extra charge. Mexes watch their step down here. Olivera Street it ain't. Me, I don't care one way or the other, long as you behave. The Shep's a residence hotel, not a barrio. *Comprende?*"

"*Comprendo.* You like this with all your check-ins?"

"Meaning what exactly?"

"This...thorough." Less backtrack than thinking about me out there on that hot pavement again. What I told myself, anyway.

He cracked a smile that showed gold and slid me a key. "Name's Lavelle. Equal opportunity hardass and ex-bouncer, so we understand each other. And the lift's currently under repair." Pointing at the elevator sign, then at one marked Stairs.

I turned from him, bent to my army duffel.

"What bean field you out of, anyway?"

"Colorado."

"Here on business?"

"I'd better be," I said, heading for the stairs.

* * *

Fourth floor—down a hall smelling like the carpet looked. Doors surrounded by outsize moldings with old-fashioned transoms. Heat bringing out everything you'd expect in a thirty-eight-year-old building without air-conditioning. "Great Balls of Fire" leaking out of the room across from mine as I pushed inside to old cigarettes, disinfectant, canned-soup smell. Iron-frame bed with a cheap gold spread, corner sink and medicine chest, worn maple easy chair and dresser, framed photo prints over it and the bed.

Poppies on the Ridge Route.

Death Valley at sunset.

First thing I did was force open the window and stick my head out over 12th Street. Traffic sounds rose and, of course, the heat. I was squaring away my things when I heard, "Good luck finding a breeze," above Conway Twitty singing "It's only Make Believe." Turning, I saw a skinny guy, taller than my five-nine. Door behind him open as mine, the room different but the same. He wore a white tee with a pack of Raleigh's rolled in the sleeve, blue jeans rolled up over white socks and black bombers. Black ducktail and sallow skin, blue eyes behind black-rimmed glasses. Jack Kerouac meets Buddy Holly.

"Ninety in December—where else but L.A.? I'm Carston Rainwater, professional n'er-do-well. Who you be?"

"Vasconsalles, Gabriel," I said in army reflex.

"Like the angel?"

"Like Gabe." Returning an unexpectedly strong handshake. Noting also that behind the glasses, where the lines lived, he had me by a good ten years. "That you across the hall?"

"Till I get a few things licked," he said. "Let me guess: Small towner sees future, leaves on next bus out, sweetheart crying in the dust. Close?"

"Try throwing rocks and you might be."

"Sorry, I'm pathologically inquisitive. Comes from trying to be Hamlet in a movie town."

"Stage actor?"

"Pathetic, huh? I never could tell west from east."

"*Sounds* exciting."

"You want to get a bite later? I know a half-decent cafeteria."

I guess he saw it in my eyes: hundred and twenty gone, one-eighty to go, L.A. on six bucks a day. What I faced breaking out like a sweat.

"No problem," he said. "Another time. You got something lined up?"

"Sort of. I have a letter."

His exit wink was knowing. "Don't we all," he said.

I'd finished my last frijole sandwich from home and was dozing despite the swelter, echoes of my family's yells and screams fading into the street hum, when I heard the knock. I opened to find him standing there, lit cigarette dangling from his lips, Brando style.

"Extras taking up space," he said, talking around it. Hot plate and a dented aluminum saucepan he handed me. "Live it up, just not around Lavelle. And bang after your interview, I'll introduce you around. Some real characters living here."

"Thanks," I said before I could add that I'd had my fill of characters for a while. My cousin with the pachuco blade for one—after I'd caught him with my eleven-year-old niece.

Make that a long while.

I woke up to my tinny Westclox, Ricky Nelson and Carston Rainwater in duet..."Poor Little Fool." Morning sun lancing in my window along with the transit noises.

I did push-ups and sit-ups, showered down the hall, put on my shirt and tie, my only slacks, then squeezed back into my oxfords, wondering how they'd gotten so small. Not wanting to interrupt Carston and the Everly Brothers now, I got Lavelle to help me with a bus route to the *Herald-Examiner* building.

I was waiting with a half-dozen other young men, all of us eyeing each other, when the door opened and a bored-sounding secretary had me follow her to a smaller office where a man sat behind a metal desk. *Sydney Blumberg* on a triangular name plate.

Topping a spread of papers was the form I'd filled out earlier and given to the secretary. Also the letter he'd sent to Pueblo in response to my query about work.

"Give me a reason," he said without looking up.

"Sir, I'm a good worker, sir."

Tired eyes met mine.

"I mean, I work hard."

"We're talking about writing, Mr. Vasconsalles. You know how to write?"

"On my base paper. In the Army. Second stint. It's on the form."

"Right, you and Elvis." He looked me up and down, during which I tried not to look away.

"Anything else?" he finally said.

"Yes, sir, there is." Wondering what it was.

"Well...?"

"Sir, I can't go back." Which surprised even me.

There was a faint nod. "You've tried the *Times*?"

"I heard don't bother unless you fit their profile."

His eyes stayed on mine. "What about the *Mirror*?"

"I want to work at a newspaper, Mr. Blumberg. A real one. Learn from the ground up."

"What makes you think I'd hire you?"

Feeling the horse I was on sweeping past the brass ring, I said, "My sergeant was Jewish, sir, the one I wrote for, the one who encouraged me. No offense, I just thought you—"

"None taken. And can that line, it cheapens you." He jotted something on the form. "Working holidays a problem?"

I saw my last Christmas at home, my mother taking the tree down with her before the old man took off his belt and really started in. The night he broke my nose.

"Definitely not."

"Know what a night owl is?"

"Sir, whatever it is, I'm your man."

"Don't make me regret it. And quit calling me sir."

* * *

Two-fifty a month to assist a staffer with police calls: One day in town, two weeks before Christmas, I actually had a job with a future. On my way back, I didn't even *see* the baked-on dirt, the brown air and diffused sun. Just stores like Orbach's and Broadway displaying sport coats, suits, and topcoats. Wondering how I'd look in one.

Approaching The Shepherd, I glanced up and saluted the angels, thought I saw one wink back at me. Carston's door was open a crack so I tapped and, in my enthusiasm, let myself in.

Teach me, I thought, exiting about as fast.

He'd been sitting in his darker version of my maple chair, a look on his face that could only be described as rapt. Like a lover who can't bear the uncoupling, he hadn't even set down the spike.

"So—when do you start?" he said later in my room, eyes still soft and dreamy. Same outfit as before, but the T-shirt damp under the arms, his odor right at home with the rest of my ghost aromas. No mention of my intrusion.

"Tonight, I said. "Twenty-two hundred to oh-four hundred."

"The witching hours. When the Jabberwock feeds, and there is the gnashing of teeth."

Nothing if not dramatic. But that was Carston.

"I suppose."

"Best time to see the city. Like now to introduce you to some of The Shepherd's flock. Come on."

Two doors down, Carston knocked and a leathery faced man with a throat scar answered, cigarette going under his squint at us, the smell of pork and beans warmer than his look. That is, until he saw Carston.

"Dodge Earle, Gabe Vasconsalles," Carston said.

We shook hands and he let us into a room so filled with empty cans and unwashed dishes, magazines and newspapers, roach killer and mousetraps, rusted folding chairs and things in cartons, we could hardly sit. But we introduced and talked awhile, Dodge in a voice that said whiskey and stogies and hard roads. Indeed, he'd been a trucker: Abilene to Oklahoma City to Denver to Salt Lake to L.A. before a heart attack put a stop to it.

"Got me sons out on the plains," he said. "Four of 'em hatin' my guts for leavin' mama. Hooch and women..." Touching the scar at my glance, he added, "This come in a bar fight in West Texas. Nineteen-forty-nine."

Carston winked on his folding chair. "Shoulda seen the other guy, right?"

"Not hardly. Hit his head and cost me a year in Wichita Falls." He eyed me and said, "So you joined our foreign legion, did you?"

I explained: Pueblo, no going home, wanting to be a reporter someday. Starting tonight.

Dodge coughed, pinned me with a look as a finch or something stirred in a cage I hadn't even noticed. "Nice spot, Colorado. And Sam over there likes the *Herald* better'n I do. Anybody else want a snort?"

"Miles to go before we drink," Carston said. And after we'd left, "Alkies and loners, grifters and dopers, all of us bound for the fair." Pausing outside a door at the end of the hall. "They're tearing it down, you know. In spring. A parking lot or some such."

I looked at him, his hand poised to knock, "Catch a Falling Star" coming up faint from downstairs. "Where will you—" Editing myself in time to make it, "Where will they go?"

The hand dropped, twitched once. "This here's The Shepherd, laddie," he said without turning. "The curb before the gutter."

The woman who answered the door when Carston got around to knocking—Rose DeChampagne he called her—was in her sixties. Minimum. Overrouged, overlipsticked, overstuffed, she saw me gawking at her, but simply gave Carston a kiss and ushered us in to 1890.

Mostly she'd done it with shawls and antimacassars, drapes and fringed throws and milk glass, things Carston had scrounged up. The whole place smelling like the rose water she wore. At her chair by the window, pair of old binoculars on the sill, she sat florid and wheezing as I went through my story again. Trying to make it sound interesting and thinking I'd have to do better as a newsman.

"How nice for you to find work," she said with a spritz of drawl. "People together in a common cause."

"Our Rose suffers from asthma," Carston said in a courtly voice. "We run out and get her things while she keeps an eye on us."

"I'm sure Mr. Vasconsalles has plenty to think about without adding me to his list."

"Gabe—please," I said. "And feel free to impose anytime. I'd be upset if you didn't."

"A southern gentleman," she said, happily. "Never ever enough of them around."

"Asthma and cheap champagne," Carston said after a half-hour had lapsed and we'd eased out. "DeChampagne's what I call her because it's where her checks mostly go."

I looked at him heading for the stairs.

"Guilt money her husband sends after marrying her AA sponsor. Her real name's Grace—Stedmon or Steptoe, something equally unfitting. You ready for the émigré who fought with Tito, the macaroni painter, and the cabbie who squashed the nun?"

Pavel Pridikov was the émigré, a burly man with wiry hair and a fondness for schnapps served twice daily—as Carston put it, day and night. He'd come to work the high iron, but while loaded had caused another man to fall ten floors onto South Broadway. End of story. He answered in his undershirt, fifty-pound free weight he'd been curling in his other hand. Between his sweat and Carston's, I barely stuck it out.

Wendell Teague, who'd also painted the lobby dunes, was a pinched-faced man surrounded by his renditions of L.A. landmarks. At least I assumed that was what they were. Easels and paints, jarred brushes, dust-covered trophies from his high school cross-country days. Photo of a laughing Adlai Stevenson, Enrico Caruso collection next to a carton of macaroni-and-cheese boxes. Disability for a nervous condition, Carston explained—forty-seven going on sixty.

Finally, we popped in on third-floor Roland Spivek, who'd cabbed the nun in a crosswalk at twilight. Twilight for him, it also happened: empty fifth of muscatel and four undisclosed DUIs adding up to six months off for good behavior and The Shepherd. A balding man with big hands and eyes that never quite engaged yours, he seemed unwilling to let me in, even with Carston there. But then he loosened enough to talk about the Catholic relief agency where he now worked, the symmetry nothing on which I cared to comment.

The opposite, in fact.

Feeling like a man in need of it, I begged off from Carston and went to my room to rest up for the night.

The reporter's name was Poole, and it didn't take him long to decide he didn't like the idea. Or maybe it was just my impression. That and the way he called me Pancho.

At any rate, he led me to a map of our territory, then around the newsroom as he one-eared the calls. Reporters pounding typewriters even at that hour, files lining the walls, an exhilarating disarray linked by fluorescent lighting and the smell of cigarettes. About eleven, after lining my questions back at me—lots of yeses and noes—we set out in his Ford with the scanner under the dash and went to work. First, a multi-stabbing outside a nightclub, back to the office to write it up, me watching and bringing him coffee. Out after midnight to a warehouse fire already extinguished, Poole nodding in mutual disgust to a *Times* guy who'd also showed. Then a strong-arm robbery and rough-up at an all-night diner, Poole extorting a sandwich as he chatted up the cops and victims.

Leaning against his Ford while he used the men's room, monitoring the box and shivering, I remember being struck by two things about L.A. One, December could be plenty cool at night, no matter how warm the day. Misleading in that respect. And two, its sheer size—beyond anything I'd expected. Like the ocean fronting it, a sea of lights and buildings, streets and cars and people...on and on, making me want to view it from the air. Vowing when I got some bucks together I'd do just that.

You see, despite Poole, I was running on pure adrenaline: that night, the rest of the week and the one heading into Christmas.

Which brings us to Madelena Rubio.

It was a Wednesday—Poole reading the ticker and me figuring everybody'd packed it in—when I heard the call. Some woman they were tending to on 12th Street.

"Isn't that us?" I asked Poole. Checking the map and matching the numbers to my block.

"Don't sound like news to me," he came back. "Besides, we're off in a half-hour."

"It's where I live, is all."

"Well whoop-de-doo. Looking to head out early, are we?"

"No, I just—"

"Aw, hit it, Pancho, get out of here. Have a taco and buzz me if it's anything."

"Sure it's okay?"

"Go on, *vamoose.*"

I was dust before he'd finished botching the word. Hitching a ride with one of the delivery trucks and thinking, *Out on my own—hot damn. So this is what it's going to be like.* Two blocks from where I could see the flashing lights after the driver let me off, I realized how close to home I was.

How close *she* was.

RUBIO, MADELENA, the younger of the two cops spelled it off the form. "*Puta,*" the older one added as we waited for the ambulance. "Beaten and robbed and who knows what. Can't even speak the language." Shaking his head. "Not that she'd talk to us anyhow."

If that didn't seal it for me, the sounds she was making did. Soft moans reminiscent of my mother's —my sister's when it got bad. From where she lay bleeding, I figured she could look up at The Shepherd's glowing letters. That is, if she could see through the swollen red things her eyes had become.

Call me a fool, but I rode the ambulance to the hospital. Waited for a nurse to give me the word as dawn lit the emergency room windows.

"The Rubio girl," she said. "You the one waiting?"

"Thought I might be of help translating."

"If she does talk to us, we have someone who *hablas Espanol*, thanks. Relative?"

I nodded—*welcome to the news brotherhood.* Besides, most things were relative. "Can I see her?"

"It's your stomach."

She did look bad: wide face, wider from the swelling, and bandaged; one eye sheathed in a taped-on patch, the other ointmented but open. Blood still caked in her hair and nose. Country girl, I guessed as her one eye tracked me crossing to it.

"How you feeling?" I asked her in Spanish.

Nothing.

"I'm not the police."

"Why you here, then?" she said. "You from Felix?"

"Felix—he your man?"

"Maybe, maybe not. If you're not the cops, who are you?"

"Name's Vasconsalles—Gabe. I'm a newspaper man."

"Got nothing to say to you or the cops. When I'm getting out of here? You know that much?"

"Nope. Sorry."

"Not as sorry as me," she said.

The nurse ran me out, and for reasons unclear to this day, I stuck around. Coffee, a thing of peanuts, and some pretzels from a vending machine. Far as I could tell from my vantage point, no cops came to question her, no other visitors. Just before two, I saw her wheeled out and met her beyond the glass front doors.

"You're looking for action, I'm out of service," she said when she saw me, her clothes still blood-spotted.

"You always this tough?"

"What do you think?"

"I think you could use a friend."

Farm girl, she finally admitted over a milk shake at Woolworth's, "Here Comes Santa Claus" playing on speakers over the counter. Weeks since she'd seen Felix, the brother she'd come up from Sonora with, both sending money home when they could. Working Lower Hope, she'd lost her night's earnings and more...virtually everything she'd made.

To *them*.

Three of them.

"You know their names?"

"The leader, I do: Antonio. And I ain't the only girl been beat on and got her money stole."

"There've been others?"

"Four I know about."

"The cops know it?"

"Like they care. Like I wouldn't be on a southbound two minutes after opening my mouth."

I twirled my straw, hoping the silence might draw her out. Or maybe because I'd run out of questions.

"They never got reported, the four I mean. I just got nailed 'cause I couldn't get up. And I gotta hit the ladies room."

I should have known she'd cut out on me.

Three days later, coming home from another night with Poole—who just shrugged when I told him about it—I couldn't sleep and started walking. Widening my radius from The Shepherd until I spotted her, the eye patch anyway, I caught up as she was heading for a stairwell. Down where the neighborhood became bars, pawnshops, warehouses.

"Trying to scare me to death?" she said in her border accent.

"Just wondered if you'd seen Antonio and his pals."

"Who's gonna do something about it if I did? You?"

"Me and the cops."

"*Mi amigos*, right. Look, I'm tired and I hurt. You want anything from me, flash it or forget it. Gabe, or whatever your name is."

"You don't care about putting these guys in jail?"

"Sure. And Santa'll be along any day now."

"Back to Antonio," I said. "You have seen him?"

She took a deep breath, touched the patch with the tips of her fingers. Then she pulled it off.

I blinked first: the eye was hideous, awash in red.

"If I tell you, will you leave me alone?"

Antonio worked in a two-story structure with loading ramps within sight of her loft. Knowing she had no choice but to keep hooking, he'd leave her alone until she earned more money she was afraid to leave in the room she shared with two other girls, then he'd hit her again.

Why not if no one spoke up?

"It's a story," I insisted to Mr. Blumberg next morning after waiting for him. Explaining Poole's unwillingness to speak about it beyond a grunt.

Mr. Blumberg unscrewed his thermos cup, poured coffee diluted with milk and sipped it. "To you, maybe," he said, setting it aside. "Which brings up a point—witnesses. You say the girl won't single them out?"

"Can you blame her? They'd kill her."

He lowered his eyes to the pen he was now rotating in both hands like a cigar. "Let me acquaint you with the facts of life, Don Quixote. You have A: no cop support I can determine, B: no angle for readership, C: no chance. Sound about right?"

"And if the cops knew it was more than an isolated incident?"

"Sometimes that's just the way it is."

"You don't believe that," I said when he finally looked up at me.

"Go home, get some sleep."

"Yes, *sir.*"

I'd turned for the door, when he said, "That hotel you listed as your address, shame about its coming down. Used to be a real anchor down there." He clunked the pen in a drawer and slid it shut. "Hell—next thing you know, it'll be newspapers."

"A *hooker*?" LaVelle said when I'd asked for help in a citizen's arrest, something I'd learned about in dealing with my family. In this case, Antonio and his *compas*. "I got enough trouble keeping the *putas* out of here—them and the dope peddlers. You even notice that? No, I didn't think so. Damn guardhouse lawyers."

As he ranted, heads raised among the chairs, turned our way, just as quickly disengaged. Back to the dust floating in the shafts of sun, the palm tree, Wendell's sand dune painting.

Desert islands, it occurred to me...like the rooms, each with its own Robinson Crusoe. Not that it was different with Dodge, Pavel, Wendell, Roland. I'd already spoken with and been turned down by them. And by Carston, who'd blown smoke and laughed.

"You think too much of us, bucko. Way too much. Despite everything you see, you think our kites are still tethered. Look again, before we soar away, dragging our broken strings behind us."

"But if what you say is true about The Shepherd," I countered, "you might be out there, too. Out where *they* are. Doesn't that mean anything to you?"

"Only to make sure it doesn't come to that," he said reaching for his spoon and syringe. "Sorry to disappoint you, Angel Gabriel, but we're experts in the field. Just ask us."

At her chair by the window...
While she keeps an eye on us...
"You're my last hope, Rose," I said as she opened the door.

"Been a long while since anybody's thought of me in those terms, Mr. Vasconsalles—Gabe," as she assumed her chair and I pulled over a re-covered stool.

Below us sounds of traffic, a streetcar, jackhammers, shouts filtered up through the week's seventy-degree air. As if it were another city as well as another time, thanks to Rose DeChampagne and her room.

She looked at me expectantly.

I said, "Five nights ago a girl was beaten and robbed down there and nobody cares."

She followed my point, settled back, let out a sigh. "Would you like a glass of water?" she asked.

"No, thanks. Would you?"

"If you'd be so kind."

After I fetched it and she'd had some, we sat watching the street, my impatience growing as my hope dimmed.

At length she said, "I haven't been outside The Shepherd in four years. What must it be like to have your whole life ahead of you?"

"Silver Bells" floated in from somewhere.

Not sure how to answer, I didn't.

"I used to know," she said. "But at that age one isn't conscious of much. I say it only because I want you to understand something."

"Understand what, ma'am?"

"That caring might not be the issue. More like what's beyond your walls is too much to bear. Inside them, even."

"One person's walls, another's window," I said. "You saw it, didn't you?"

Tears filled her eyes, and she nodded. "Three of them, red bandannas on their heads. And I did nothing. What they did to that poor defenseless girl..."

She put out a hand and I took it.

"It's not over yet," I said, unpocketing my notebook and pencil.

* * *

Mr. Blumberg was at lunch, so I dropped Rose's statement along with a note from me in his box. *Worth a try*, I thought. Which led me to slide one under Carston's door as well: where I was going, what I had planned, where to send my personal effects. Kidding, in a way.

Lavelle said, "Hey, wanna talk to you," as I made my way through the lobby, but I didn't stop. At four-thirty it was already getting dark, and the half-hour it took to Antonio's warehouse made it that much darker. Colder. Stationed where I was by the ramps, I wondered if Madelena Rubio was getting ready to hit the streets, or if she was already there.

Five-thirty came and went, then an exodus of employees—hard-looking types who dispersed with an unbowed physical grace. I was about to give it up when they bounced outside, the door slamming shut behind them. Red bandannas, blue jeans, heavy shoes. Long-sleeved shirts buttoned to the neck.

Now or never, I told myself, pushing off from the streetlight.

"Antonio," I called.

"Who wants him?" the tallest one said, peering at me. "I know you?"

"No, but I know you. The *puto* so tough he hurts women for their night money."

For a moment Antonio stared. Then he laughed, slapped hands with the other two.

"Hurt 'em cause I like it, *Vato*. And the money's mine, less you want some, too. Then we got a problem."

"Not here for money," I said. "I'm here to warn you."

"To warn me... Just you..."

More laughs, the two beginning to flank me as if he'd signaled them.

"I work for the *Herald-Examiner*. Right now there's a witness statement on my editor's desk. Unless you back off, the cops get it. *Comprende?*"

"How 'bout we kill your witness, then your whore, then you *madre?*" No cars, nobody on the street—just pools of light, shadow, fear. The two fanned out to where I had to take my eyes off Antonio to see them.

"After we kill you."

And suddenly it was another face I saw. *HIS* face. Before the sheet covered it and they wheeled it away and my mother came at me with fists and nails as I held up the bloody boxing weight I'd used to defend myself from him. *HIS* face. Toppling into the mud from its gravesite easel, trampled there by the brawl that proved a fitting tribute.

MY FATHER'S face.

Which is when they hit me, of course, solid blows despite my own. Then stood me up for Antonio's brass knuckles.

Everything was going red-blind, my knees sagging, jaw hanging slack, when they let me drop. But instead of getting their feet into me, they backed off. And there seemed to be more feet. Two-by-fours connecting, sounds only I was making moments before.

Then somebody—Carston, I took it—saying, "Don't die on us now, Macbeth."

Lavelle shouting, "Get that mother up, Dodge, I ain't done yet."

"Don't kill them," I remember mouthing as the sirens closed in. "We need them alive."

Not only did our citizen's arrest stick, six girls plus Madelena came forward to identify Antonio and his thugs. Strength in numbers. Mr. Blumberg ran a story on it—small, but better than nothing. Christmas Eve morning he actually left me a note to hang around, then bought me breakfast.

"Time to spread your wings a little, don't you think?" he said over lox and bagels, a first for me. In fact, I thought that was what he was referring to. But then he said, "I want to follow up the basic we ran. Different slant: good citizens going out of their way to help. Put the hotel in the middle of it. The one they're pulling down without a full hearing. Got it?"

"I think so, sir."

"Thought we had an understanding about that."

"Mr. Blumberg."

"Good, because you're writing it."

* * *

That night, led by Madelena Rubio, the oddest collection of short-skirted, candle-holding angels sang carols in Spanish outside our windows. Fringed shawls and white-lace *rebozos* over their working garb, they sang "*El Tamborilero...Blanca Navidad...Noche de Paz.*" Right out of my childhood, not a dry eye in the house. Lavelle even let them sing in the lobby, where a *Herald* photographer took the group shot that ran with my article. Which went a long way toward getting The Shepherd permanently acquired by the Housing and Redevelopment Agency.

No wrecking ball.

As for me, Mr. Blumberg advanced me the money to fly home for New Year's, the lights seeming to stretch clear to Pueblo. Where for once the family Vasconsalles made peace instead of war. But I didn't live there anymore. I lived in L.A. And every time I passed that old pile of bricks—long after I moved out and Rose became an angel herself—I'd salute the cherubs and thank whatever'd led me to Carston, Dodge, Wendell, Roland, Lavelle...

All of us who found ourselves at The Shepherd.

OTHER TITLES FROM DOWN AND OUT BOOKS

By J. L. Abramo
Catching Water in a Net
Clutching at Straws
Counting to Infinity
Gravesend

By Trey R. Barker
2,000 Miles to Open Road
Road Gig: A Novella
Exit Blood (*)

By Richard Barre
The Innocents
Bearing Secrets
Christmas Stories
The Ghosts of Morning
Blackheart Highway
Burning Moon
Echo Bay (*)
Lost *)

By Milton T. Burton
Texas Noir

By Reed Farrel Coleman
The Brooklyn Rules

By Don Herron
Willeford (*)

By Terry Holland
An Ice Cold Paradise
Chicago Shiver
Warm Hands, Cold Heart (*)

By David Housewright & Renée Valois
The Devil and the Diva

By David Housewright
Finders Keepers

By Valester Jones
The Pimp and the Gangster (*)

By Jon Jordan
Interrogations

By Jon & Ruth Jordan
Murder and Mayhem in Muskego
(Editors)

By Bill Moody
Czechmate: The Spy Who Played Jazz
Fair Trade (*)

By Gary Phillips
The Perpetrators
Scoundrels: Tales of Greed, Murder
and Financial Crimes (Editor)

By Lono Waiwaiole
Wiley's Lament
Wiley's Shuffle
Wiley's Refrain
Dark Paradise

(*)—Coming Soon